Survive

Survive

Frederika Amalia Finkelstein

TRANSLATED BY ISABEL COUT
AND CHRISTOPHER ELSON

DEEP VELLUM PUBLISHING
DALLAS, TEXAS

Deep Vellum Publishing
3000 Commerce Street, Dallas, Texas 75226
deepvellum.org · @deepvellum

Deep Vellum is a 501c3 nonprofit literary arts organization founded in 2013
with the mission to bring the world into conversation through literature.

Support for this publication has been provided in part by grants from the National
Endowment for the Arts, the Texas Commission on the Arts, the City of Dallas Office of
Arts and Culture, the Communities Foundation of Texas, and the Addy Foundation.

Paperback ISBN: 9781646053049
Ebook ISBN: 9781646053193

LIBRARY OF CONGRESS CATALOGING-IN-PUBLICATION DATA

Names: Finkelstein, Frederika Amalia, author. | Cout, Isabel, translator. |
Elson, Christopher, 1965- translator.
Title: Survive / Frederika Amalia Finkelstein ; translated by Isabel Cout
and Christopher Elson.
Other titles: Survivre. English
Description: Dallas, Texas : Deep Vellum Publishing, 2024.
Identifiers: LCCN 2024011139 (print) | LCCN 2024011140 (ebook) | ISBN
9781646053049 (trade paperback) | ISBN 9781646053193 (ebook)
Subjects: LCGFT: Psychological fiction. | Novels.
Classification: LCC PQ2706.I557 S8713 2017 (print) | LCC PQ2706.I557
(ebook) | DDC 843/.92--dc23/eng/20240313
LC record available at https://lccn.loc.gov/2024011139
LC ebook record available at https://lccn.loc.gov/2024011140

Cover art and design by Daniel Gray
Interior layout and typesetting by Andrea García Flores

Printed in the United States of America

Introduction

In *Survive*, Frederika Amalia Finkelstein's second novel and the second novel we have had the privilege of translating together, the author returns to the unsettling and complex questions of her first novel, *Forgetting*, with new insight and maturity. Though not twins, these novels share a deep affinity and a resonance, as they question how individuals, especially young people, navigate the quest for personal meaning and fulfillment in a late-stage capitalist world torn apart by constant violence. What we called in the Introduction to *Forgetting* (2014) "the warring imperatives to remember and to forget" are also experienced and examined further in *Survive*. The ghostly and temporally removed violence of the Holocaust that haunts Finkelstein's first novel gives way to the disturbingly bloody present: the transformed French social and cultural context of the November 13, 2015, terrorist attacks in Paris and their wide-ranging ramifications.

Survive is written in the voice of the "Bataclan Generation," named for the concert venue where the highest number of victims perished on that night of multiple attacks. It is a generation born of a single event. Not an unforeseeable event, perhaps, given the attacks on *Charlie Hebdo* in January of the same year, but nevertheless an unimaginable event rendered horribly concrete, undeniable in the sheer fact of its occurrence. Finkelstein, in a writerly project that is proving itself to be fearlessly and worryingly consistent, takes up the task of speaking of and to this event. In pages haunted by what she repeatedly refers to as "the November dead," the young author does not turn away from what she calls "a duty to look them in the eyes."

The theme of sight, especially as it pertains to the question of bearing witness to brutality and misery, is particularly central for the author. Finkelstein approaches it from many angles: there is a photograph of a dead body as well as the online circulation of a snuff-film, and the questions of self-(re)presentation in the online space and of literal sightlessness as the narrator, a voyeur who finds herself compulsively looking, envies the almost heightened perceptiveness of her blind younger sister. The question of whether it is better to look or not look is central—is it more insulting to blur the body, thereby insinuating that death has an nearly pornographic quality, or more insulting to expose it to the gaze, to render it absolutely and helplessly vulnerable? The narrator inhabits a world of daily live streams, endlessly shared and re-shared across the anarchy of the internet, of what "the public never should have seen."

Offered early and offered bluntly, Finkelstein's descriptions of the various concatenations of violated flesh and the meeting of bodies shattered by the weapons of terrorist violence are remarkable in their intensity—sometimes clinically distant, sometimes emotionally uncontainable. The body is so central here and Finkelstein writes the body in its contemporary situation like few others. There cannot be many texts of narrative fiction that portray the new intersections between the human and the technical, between the device and the body, as pertinently or as pointedly as Finkelstein's novels. What we might call an emergent trans-human interface is repeatedly drawn out at the same time that the timeless, ahistorical human vulnerability of our singular embodiment is explored unflinchingly, right up to its most gruesome ends and, very daringly, beyond them.

This novel situates contemporary youth in a violence-saturated present with which they are all too familiar. Exposure through the internet to graphic images and videos of violence, suffering, and loss has ceased to be the exception and is now a fundamental aspect of contemporary human experience. For

Finkelstein's anti-heroic narrator, Ava, a Western youth who enjoys the relative safety of the "First World," "the hardest thing, the cruelest thing [is] . . . to keep trying to be shocked by these things." An uphill battle rages in Ava to maintain empathy, to maintain a sense of global, shared humanity beyond brutality, and to navigate the increasingly blurred boundaries between the everyday and moments of historical crisis or emergency.

Finkelstein provides a glimpse of the challenge facing her generation to understand their own lives as uniquely meaningful in the face of what seems like unending mass suffering. "I'm under twenty-five and I am unable to envision the future. I'm not the only one," she writes. This struggle to project into a future menaced by the ever-looming threat of political, public health, and climate crises eats away at the individual already trying to cope with the anxieties of the everyday: *Am I successful enough, beautiful enough, interesting enough? Is my life meaningful enough?* These two parallel sources of fear (the fear of violence, suffering, and loss alongside the fear of failing to meet society's expectations) operate on different registers and compete for Ava's attention as she hovers, undecided, between redoubling her efforts to do what is expected of her, and abandoning it all: "I told myself there was no place for me here . . . I felt worthless, like I was nothing . . . I kept dreaming of a destiny: leave, start over." This is the paradox at the heart of *Survive*: while Ava's obsession with violence and death appears to be eating away at her, it might actually be a balm to soothe other inescapable and mundane anxieties. Indeed, as Ava says while looking at the photograph on her wall of the bodies strewn across the floor of the Bataclan, "every anxiety becomes ludicrous: I tell myself very simply that I am lucky to be alive." She finds a bizarre but deeply human comfort in that, in simply feeling lucky to be alive, no longer forced to contemplate the questions of meaning or destiny so characteristic of young adulthood.

Many passages of this compact narrative show the author's extraordinary capacity to represent our multiple fragilities and our refracted belonging to flesh, to culture, to history, to technology, to ideas—to life and death, to remembering and to forgetting. The imperative to survive (an imperative that we as translators have chosen to emphasize grammatically by making an imperative of the infinitive verb that is the book's French title, *Survivre*) means somehow gathering all these aspects of being human despite the looming possibility of their definitive effacement, alteration, uncontrollable metamorphosis, or downright oblivion (another possible translation of *Forgetting*'s French title, *L'oubli*). As readers and critics, we see clearly that for Finkelstein, no synthesis or reordering of these elements is guaranteed or, indeed, necessarily desirable.

But there is here, as in the first of the two related novels, a desire for awakening and even, in *Survive*, a conviction expressed in the very last words of the text that such an awakening is happening, possible in spite of everything that works against it, denies it, overwhelms it. For Finkelstein, it is essential "[t]o abide. Deep inside what is dying . . . to build a world that thinks, a world that gives, a world that beats—a living world."

—Isabel Cout and Christopher Elson

2024

You want a world. That's why you have
everything and you have nothing.
FRIEDRICH HÖLDERLIN

I don't know how to make it through:
I'll make it through anyway.
ARTHUR RIMBAUD

In reality, that which is irrational and which has no
explanation is not evil—on the contrary: it is good.
IMRE KERTÉSZ

I

1

I never believed in a better world, but this violence we're living—in France, in Europe—this violence is killing me.

It's 7:44 AM, I'm on the platform of Stalingrad Station. A squad of four soldiers has just stopped beside me. I close my eyes and try to think of something beautiful: I see my childhood home again, its garden brimming with flowers (hortensias, lilacs, daisies), its blue shutters edged with rust and its walls turned scaly by the ocean's salt. I reopen my eyes: one of the soldiers cradles his gun in the crook of his arm, barrel pointed at my stomach. It would only take a fit of madness—for just one of them to be overcome—and we'd all be dead. I take a big step back. An odor of rubber and burnt metal invades the station, followed by a shrill, piercing sound as the wheels scrape against rails. The ground shakes a little. I want to order that soldier to stop pointing his weapon at me, but I don't dare speak to him; I don't want to get into a conflict with authority, even less so with individuals armed with weapons of war. Who knows what could happen, they look just as nervous as me.

Unload your weapon, I want to yell. *Empty it, don't humiliate me.*

The train pulls into the station and passes before my eyes. It stops, the doors open. Dozens of people disappear into the contradiction of the crowd. So many people I'll never know. So many people I'll never see again. I wait until the car empties and then I get on. The soldiers stay on the platform—a relief. The crowd jostles me. All the seats in the car are occupied. I position myself near a metal bar to hold on to in case they slam on the brakes suddenly.

I stare and they stare back. Breaths mingle; bodies touch. This forced intimacy is an ordeal. I can count nine women, twelve men, three children. There are shirts, tracksuits, fake leather jackets, T-shirts, wireless headphones, screens held in hands. I close my eyes again, I try to return to the garden of my childhood home. That memory has the power to soothe me for a handful of moments. I make abundant use of it, but it doesn't take much for the bitterness to seep back in (we had to sell the house and we walked away with almost nothing). I pat down my pockets. My fingers feel the edges of a rectangular form. It's not a book;

it's my phone. I thought I brought a book this morning. I was wrong.

Twelve stations and I can get off. The train begins to move. The eyes around me are switched off and ringed with bags. To my left—the ends of her hairbrush against my elbow, her perfume is sour—is a woman between twenty-five and thirty-five (I couldn't give you an exact number), engrossed by her phone screen. Her pupils wander from left to right, never stopping, the thumb of her right hand scrolling across the surface of her device with a mix of agitation and fluidity. I'm almost moved by this symbiosis of human and machine—though the term "emotion" is maybe not quite right: it's more like a kind of ever-renewing surprise. I screw up my eyes and stare at her screen (she's small so I'm able to make out the news over her shoulder). I read: *The battle rages. Civilians are massacred. It will be a matter of hours before the regime regains control of the city. Families are trapped. Children are being killed in the street. All the hospitals have been destroyed. Impossible to recover the bodies. Impossible to escape. The streets are open graves. The deluge of bombs and heavy artillery is incessant. It's the last phase of the war.*

The young woman has just paused the movement of her thumb. She clicks on a news article. The page takes a moment to load. I feel an extreme tiredness, very briefly, like a dizzy spell. The page has loaded, the sentences now spread across the page. Many numbers appear in quick succession. The words "wounded" and "dead" are repeated. It's about an attack, I don't know where it happened, not that the location really matters. I skim the contents of the article efficiently. A quarter of the wounded seem to be in very bad shape ("extreme critical condition" is the official term). The final count of victims is provisional: the seriously wounded might at any moment need to be counted among the dead.

The daily barrage of mass murder always shocks me a bit, but much less than it used to. The efforts I've made to get used to it have begun to bear fruit: life must go on and we must move forward, walking over the dead. I mean to say that we have a duty to go on with our lives, and to live well, of course. If we don't step over the dead and make our way forward, they'll be the ones burying us. We'd be giving in to despair. I remember the testimony of a young man present at the November 13th attacks: he confessed to trampling a pregnant woman, without hesitation, in order to escape the terrorists' bullets. He seemed deeply troubled by his confession, but at least he told the truth. What's more, it is entirely likely that dozens of other people trampled that woman. I certainly won't be the first to cast a stone—I'd have probably done the same thing. When death swoops down before you, brushing past, only one word remains: survive. Your heart beats louder; your heart cries out against death, it cries out that it wants to live, whether or not it has to trample a woman to do so, whether or not that woman is pregnant. But worse even than despair is doubt—and it's to doubt that we succumb if we don't get used to making our way over the bodies of the dead. There's nothing more dangerous than doubt (unfortunately, I know a thing or two about it). I very nearly lost myself to doubt: I almost fell into the spiral of its madness. Be careful with it: doubt is a cancer that spreads invisibly through your body until it has exterminated even your most modest dreams.

The train stops abruptly. My right hand clutches the metal bar, and so brushes other hands. It is warm, damp, slippery, I think of the thousands (maybe even millions) of germs being spread at this very moment. Too rarely do we turn our attention to the things swarming all around us: don't they say that rats, mice, and cockroaches make up the greater part of any city's population? Germs. Insects. Rodents. Corpses. In the end, aren't they all the same? No one really likes to live among them, but we have no other choice, we have to allow them to pile up in our cities.

The young woman turns off her phone screen, she sticks it in her pocket. She sighs. I shift my attention to another screen on my right. It's true that I take advantage of public transportation to enter the lives of others:

I steal little clues about the existences of people around me, into which I'm not supposed to venture, the existences of people with whom I'll probably never rub shoulders (it's a statistical likelihood, I live in a metropolis). But even if the moment is precarious and limited, I delight in it. It's one of the minuscule joys I allow myself each morning, and I have to admit, as the years go by, I have fewer and fewer reasons to rejoice about anything in this life. So I'm learning humility. Every day: humility. The owner of the phone to which I'm absolutely riveted has just noticed my indiscretion. He turns his phone slightly toward his chest, leaving me alone in a crude reality. No point in checking my own phone. I don't have any service on line two. I've got it on line twelve, line one, and line four, but never on line two. I look at my smart watch. It's 8:10 AM—plenty of time.

Last night, I woke up sweating. I'd just had a nightmare, always the same nightmare that wakes me around 4:00 AM, and afterward, as always: impossible to fall back asleep. I went to the bathroom, I splashed cold water on my face and I locked the door. I leaned my back against the door and then I opened a book: Rimbaud's *A Season in Hell*. In that moment, I really needed it. The November dead were haunting me, always the same damn dead. There was anger deep inside me. Vile thoughts coursed through me—I was angry at life, at death, at fear, at my country, at Europe, at my phone, my computer, at the corrupt politicians, at the long, unjust, dirty wars, at my flaws, my family, the present, the past, at the terrorists and the soldiers—*they're all sick in the head,* I thought. And suddenly I thought I saw the blood of the dead running in my bathtub, I wanted to blame something, someone—after all, these daily sacrifices of men and women are nothing other than the exhibition of a crime against humanity. Yet, when I'm faced with the question of who is guilty, I still cannot answer.

I've had this nightmare regularly since I saw that sordid photograph of the pit at the Bataclan. When I picture those pierced, torn bodies, abandoned in humiliating positions, when I picture the carnage as it is in my memory: I am full of hate. When I picture the blood spread across the ground I taste metal, and it's like that blood is in my mouth, like their blood was my blood, and once again I am filled with hate. Often I tell myself I shouldn't have gone looking for that photograph. But it couldn't be helped: as soon as I knew it existed (and even more so when I learned it was forbidden to share it on social media) finding it became an obsession. Real efforts were made to prevent it from being accessed, but too many websites were circulating it, the authorities were powerless: every one hundredth of a second, the number of images multiplied and the web found itself literally flooded with copies of the photograph. So in less than a minute, I had the photograph before my eyes. But there was a problem: the bodies had been blurred, as though it was unacceptable to see them in their death; as though they were pornographic. This infuriated me because I wanted to see the bodies— more specifically, I wanted to see what had been done to them. Is the sight of a murdered body a dishonor? No—blurring the body of a dead person is to kill them a second time. I had to find an uncensored version of that photograph because I had to see those bodies in their reality, before they were violated by the propriety of the media—I had to see them as they were, innocent in death. It was a question of respect for what they had endured, and maybe also, I confess, a voyeuristic reflex.

But once again, I overestimated the threat: without any difficulty, I was able to find the unadulterated photograph, without any retouches, on the biggest social media network in the world. I was still disappointed: it wasn't high definition enough. It had been compressed, probably to make online circulation easier. So the faces were mutilated: they had become sites of vertigo, the stumbling block for the imagination.

I've said it, it's a risk, we shouldn't modify or reinvent the dead: we must resist that temptation. I downloaded the photograph all the same, initially thinking I'd store it on an external hard drive, just in case it disappeared from the internet, until I realized that this fear was completely unfounded: aside from the fact that I don't think I'll ever be able to eradicate this catastrophe from my memory, when an image appears on the internet, it's definitive: the virtual traces are ineradicable. An image strikes you, it starts to live in you, and spreads inside until it has put its roots down in your being.

What has been is and will be

Having examined it for so long, I've imprinted the photograph in my memory. The photograph has been sharpened and its details have become finer, to the point where I no longer need to have it in front of me in order to describe it. All it takes is a little concentration.

*

A person of the male sex jostles me, his black backpack knocking against my shoulder. Its fabric gives off a smell of wet stone and saltpeter, followed by the still more radical scent of deodorant. I'd better describe that photograph I'm obsessed with, if I don't do it now, it'll linger like a dark secret.

Twice I've been in that concert hall: I've been in that pit. The club's lights, the height of the stage, the color of the seats on the first balcony, I remember it all.

But what diverges considerably from my experience is most certainly the pit itself: in times past, full of people standing, pressed up against one another, dancing, shouting. It's now strewn with bleeding bodies, inert, so that what was once a mosh pit is now a mass grave. Some bodies are piled on top of one another, others are separated, alone in a corner. There are legs spread apart, dislocated wrists, sometimes bare feet. Between them, enormous bloody tracks stain the ground: the bodies themselves produced these marks—they were dragged. I know because it's as if there's something missing: too much blood for too few bodies, which makes me think that at the moment the photograph was taken, the paramedics had already removed fifty or so bodies. I want to say *cleaned up* but I'm having trouble committing to using that term, it disturbs me, it almost seems insulting even if it's accurate. Don't hold this against me, but I couldn't help myself, I went and checked the dictionary definition because I like it when words are used fittingly. The *Larousse* defines *cleaned* as: "Clean, clear, removing everything that stains, dirties, tarnishes [. . .] eliminating the undesirable, dangerous elements from a place." So like it or not, the verb *to clean* is fitting for the situation in question, for this half-emptied pit: what else are you doing when you drag a dead body away to the morgue, then put it underground, if not tidying up, clearing away, and finally, relieving the living of these bodies, the ones who were witnesses to the worst. That's also what was intended by blurring the bodies: to clean them up. But I'm losing the thread. I was saying: the paramedics had no doubt already removed at least fifty bodies by the time the photograph was taken (if my calculations are correct, given that we see twenty-eight bodies in the photo and the total body count for that room had come in at eighty-nine).

The train stops in the middle of the tunnel. The lights flicker and go out. Here we are, plunged into darkness. Everyone remains calm. *It's the final phase of the war.* It's true that things should always end on a high note: if we don't go out with a bang, victory doesn't taste as sweet. There have been too many dramas, too many fights, too much effort put into this long war for it not to go out with a bang. There always needs to be a grand finale. Pitiless, dense, burning; a grand finale like a final explosion of rebellion. The last fireworks I saw were in Venice, watching from the Giudecca. It was three years ago. It was cold and the night was pitch black. *The children of Aleppo.* The children of Aleppo: never shall they leave this earth. The dust from their bodies will seep into the earth which will bring forth flowers which will bring forth trees which will bring forth the fruits we'll eat— and so we'll eat the dead. We'll eat those children. We will eat the women violated. We will eat the fathers, the sons, the mothers, and the daughters. We will eat our shame.

The darkness persists. The passengers sigh. Anger is rising, silently. An old weariness stuffed down inside the body, unresolved, ready to announce itself.

Moving on. There are approximately twenty-eight bodies in the pit. I say *approximately* because it's possible I'm off, some remains formed into masses of flesh, which makes counting difficult: legs intertwined, arms, backs and bellies touching. I focus on the faces, if I trust in the faces it'll be impossible to miscount: one face is equal to one body. Yes, that seems obvious, but I swear to you, in this photograph the notion of a human being is not clear, and the 1:1 ratio of head to body isn't either. They are in monstrous postures, one could say they seem more like creatures endowed with what we can identify as limbs, hair, torsos, but who bear no real resemblance to the human species; one arm bent, another stretched above a head, legs curled up here and stretched long there, bellies turned toward the sky, cheeks crushed against the ground or buried in the armpit of another body.

My breath grows shallower, I can't seem to fill my lungs. The young woman on my right has just slipped on a pair of headphones. A rhythmic ternary beat plays, muffled. I casually slide my wrist a reasonable distance from my eyes and check the time on my watch. I don't want to be late for work, but if the metro doesn't start moving again in the next five minutes, it'll be unavoidable. I slide my arm back down along my side with the same deliberateness, careful not to touch anyone. The lights come back on. The train starts moving again. I'll go on. In the foreground lie eight bodies. A man, at the edge of the stage on the right, is wearing jeans and a navy-blue shirt. He's lying on his back, his legs are spread apart but his feet are together: his body forms a triangle. He wears white sneakers decorated with a large black check. His left hand rests on his abdomen. I can't see his right hand. Next to this body, I can only make out legs in a pair of faded jeans, bent in two and lying on their left side. Another young man on the ground in front of him is wearing a pair of dark jeans, a white T-shirt, and an unbuttoned plaid shirt. He has a red stain on his right side. His arms are splayed out, making a right angle, as though he'd wanted to make one last gesture before he died. His face is turned toward the ceiling, his eyes are open, they stare into nothingness while his knee touches the foot of another body, also dressed in jeans and wearing a black jacket—the face isn't visible, it's submerged in a pool of blood—as its two hands touch the two bodies beside it, themselves entwined; the head of the first, bald, leans lightly against the thigh of the second. My head is spinning, I no longer have control of my breathing—it's because of the proximity of all these other bodies, but it's okay, soon I'll be off this train (every time I'm in a crowded compartment, I think of the cattle cars used not so long ago to deport human beings). I'll go on. The first is wearing a white T-shirt, a gray hoodie tied around the waist and jeans, while the second (only partially visible) is wearing a black top and white high-top tennis shoes—I used to wear the same ones in high school. The second body's right shoe is right on the edge of the thick pool of blood, the same pool that the face of the body with the bald head is submerged in. In the center of the hall lies a group of five bodies: they seem to be embracing one another. Four pairs of legs are covered in jeans, while the fifth, on the left side, is wearing only leggings, dark and translucent, knee-high leather boots, and a black mini-skirt. That young woman isn't with the group. She's alone, so she died alone, she was slaughtered alone. I find the sight of the miniskirt unpleasant. I can't help but think if that young woman had known she was going to die that night, she'd have chosen different clothes. *To die in a miniskirt.* It's a limited thought, I'll give you that, but I couldn't stop it from forming, and what's more, I can't see the victim's face and that bothers me: it's buried in long, black hair, so much so that I'm gripped by a terrible feeling of discomfort—we can see the young woman's miniskirt but we can't see her face. This photograph will end up in archives and all that History will retain of the death of this human being is *a miniskirt without a face.*

My memory will never give her a face or a name, at least unless it invents one, but it's like I've been telling you—the dead shouldn't be retouched or modified.

Ten feet from her, on her right, a second individual lies alone. I can't even manage to tell whether it's a man or a woman. A gust of fresh air blows into the subway compartment, I reopen my eyes, I raise my head, I inhale thinly. *You've forgotten some bodies*, says a voice, the voice inside me. I abhor it. It materializes without warning and interrupts me, even goes so far as to order me around. I detest its interruptions even though I always end up obeying. Behind the two lone bodies, then, a triad is scattered across the ground: the head of the first body (furthest to the left) is pressed into the back of the second, while the third is a little off to the side, touching the second body with its left foot. He's wearing a red T-shirt, as red as the trail of blood that runs in a straight line from his face to flow subtly—yes, I'm insisting on that word, *subtle*, the trickle is neat and particularly straight—a distance of about seven or eight meters; excuse my inexactness, I've always been hopeless at geometry.

The last cluster—and the most difficult to distinguish—is in the background, to the left of the stage. It's a heap of blood-soaked flesh and clothing. Backs, buttocks, pants and shirts are visible, the edge of a slightly raised elbow, and several handfuls of hair, but here too, there are no faces. I'd have liked to know their names, to be able to associate each body with a last name and a first name. If I knew the names of each of these bodies, I could learn them by heart. I really like learning lists of names by heart, at least as much as I like learning poems.

Judging by certain items of clothing, certain faces, the youthfulness of their features, the evidence becomes irrefutable: none of these bodies is more than thirty years old. Like I told you, I don't know their names, or what they like to be called. Only the police know, only their families know, unless they are equally lost, or have deliberately chosen to remain in the dark. It must be unbearable (the word is insufficient) to see your child in such a posture.

*

I'll be honest: if I remember this photograph with such precision, it's because I printed it out and stuck it on the wall of my room above my desk. Sometimes, looking at it does me good: it reminds me of what human beings are capable of and of just how far violence can go. So, looking at it, I instantly get some perspective on how hard life is and my own situation. Standing in front of this photograph, every anxiety becomes ludicrous: I tell myself very simply that I am lucky to be alive. Horror can intrude at any time.

Disgust and anger come afterward, when I no longer have the photograph in front of me. I told you that they were haunting me, but I lied: it's me that's doing everything I can to hold onto them. That's why I followed this line of reasoning: if I'm choosing to live among them, I need to at least try to remember their faces, their last names, their first names.

So I also printed out all the faces of those who died on November 13th, as published on *Le Monde* website, and I stuck them to the wall in my room, next to the photograph of the mosh pit—the mass grave, I should say. There are ninety faces: nine rows of ten dead. Under each face I wrote in the first name, last name, and age (not the age they'd be now, but the age that they were when they died). Naturally, *What to do about the terrorists* is the question that confronted me next: part of me wanted to print out their faces and stick them to the wall, too, next to the victims (I hate that word), while another part of me furiously opposed the idea. But, having seen their faces over and over again in the media, I accepted the obvious: it's impossible to ignore the killers. So I printed their faces out and added them to the group.

I'm getting ready to thread my way through the bodies blocking the subway doors. If the words "excuse me" don't do it, I'll add a "sorry"—more effective. I tend to settle on the contents of my sentences before speaking them, it's a habit linked to excessive shyness (speaking has always been problematic, I'd even say it's always been like walking on eggshells).

I've hidden God away in a corner of my head. I've gone along like it's possible to live without ever thinking about it—without ever asking myself where the world came from. By around sixteen, I was already thinking of leaving my country. To start a life elsewhere, far from the meat grinder that is this city, far from this system of selection on the basis of numbers: always numbers. I told myself there was no place for me here. Too many sacrifices, too many injustices. And I felt worthless, like I was nothing. At the same time, I kept dreaming of a destiny: leave, start over. But a voice inside me, disenchanted, always ended up talking me out of it: saying *you waste of space, you're going to waste your life and you're going to end up alone and lost and ugly and poor, and there's nothing you can do about it: it's already too late.*

*

On that night in November, I followed it, I watched like a voyeur as it unfolded live, I was there in front of my screens like millions of others, but I wasn't there, in that room, or in those restaurants, or in those cafés, in the nerve center of the worst.

I've had my heart broken, I've felt catastrophic anguish, but I've never been present for a massacre, I've never taken a bullet and I've never endured a hostage situation: I've never paid with my own flesh, I've never paid with my life.

I should have gone to the morgue the day after the slaughter to see the sacrificed up close: I would have liked those corpses to transmit something to me, something of what they experienced—for them to have me taste, through the bruises on their skin, the emptiness of their eyes, frozen in terror, to taste just a tiny part of the ultimate hellscape they traversed.

At this moment, in the middle of this crowded subway car full of bodies ready for work just like mine, I feel linked to the dead, to their pain, and to their destiny. They are martyrs. They are heroes. Insofar as they died gratuitously. To me they have become gods—gods sullied by murder; the ones who became gods without wanting to. I think back to the photograph, to its censure. *Don't defile the dead. Let us see them.* We have a duty to look them in the eyes. The train stops, the doors open. I say "sorry" but no one hears; I say, "excuse me," and force my way through a little bit. There are days when I feel invisible, full of silent griefs.

2

You got me.

TRAYVON MARTIN, age seventeen

I come out of Charles-de-Gaulle-Étoile station. It's
8:29 AM, the temperature is twenty degrees Celsius;
my heart rate is ninety-two beats per minute (I picked
up the pace a few seconds ago and now I'm a bit out
of breath). The wafting aromas of diesel and thawing
pastries mix with the smell of chlorophyll from the
chestnut and plane trees lining the Champs-Élysées.
I stare at Qatar's red and white flag, floating supreme
from the edge of the embassy's window, facing the Arc
de Triomphe. I inhale deeply, this alloy of pollution
and damp bark signals the beginning of September.
The smell sends me back to my childhood, I'd always
take a big gulping breath before stepping through the

school gate (passing through that gate meant knowing exactly where I'd be for the next eight hours, and that restriction of my movement always engendered a gut-churning distress.

I'm a bit low today. That's how it is for me about a third of the time, maybe half the time. To ward off the anguish and melancholia, I exercise. I go running three times a week at a municipal stadium near the Porte de Pantin. I've found a way to keep the rhythm of my steps consistent: in my head, I recite long lists of the dead. More specifically, I learn lists of massacres and deadly attacks off by heart from Wikipedia, and I recite them in my head as I do laps around the track. It's no harder than learning poems, and it allows me to remove myself from the pain brought on by my exertion.

The lists are organized by time period: Antiquity, the Middle Ages, the modern era, the contemporary era, and "since 2001" (apparently September 11th was a watershed moment). Next to every event is the date, the number of victims, as well as a brief description of the event. There are several kinds of lists available: the list of massacres, the list of deadly attacks, the list of school shootings, and the list of aerial bombings. That's the good thing about these lists: they're so extensive that I have enough material for my whole run. I generally run six kilometers without stopping, so about sixteen laps around the stadium, reciting to myself the number of deaths in chronological order, from 2001 to the present. There's no point in adding that I sweat copiously, and that's no doubt why I run—it's how I cry, through the pores in my skin.

I don't know who assembled the lists, and according to which criteria. For example, the atomic bombs in Nagasaki and Hiroshima don't appear on the list of massacres: they're on the list of aerial bombings. Furthermore, the numbers vary enormously: for anything with less than a hundred victims, the phrase "several dozens" is used; on the other hand, when the exact figure is uncertain or unknown, a plus sign followed by a question mark is used, e.g., between 2007 and 2008 in Kenya violence surrounding the elections causes "+1,500?" deaths; from August 14th to 16th, the massacre that took place at Rabaa al-Adawiya leads to "~800," which is to say, about eight hundred dead. This kind of imprecision isn't easy to work with, but I make do, I have no choice: in case of any uncertainty, I settle for using one of two expressions: "about" or "more or less," followed by the official estimate of the number of deaths.

Don't think I'm lazy, and also don't be fooled by the slight interval of time that's passed since 2001 as compared to two thousand years of history. The lists from the last fifteen years are on another level compared to the ones compiling together two thousand years of history. The lists from the last decade are literally collapsing beneath all the massacres, killings and attacks: there are so many they have to be classified into subcategories: first by month, and then by day. Which brings me back to the fact that even if I wanted to, I wouldn't be able to recite the massacres from the twentieth century all in one go after having recited the important massacres of the twenty-first. The truth is, our century is so rife with massacres, killings and attacks that I've never been able to recite them all before ending my run. After sixty uninterrupted minutes of counting the mass deaths in chronological order, breathless, sweating like crazy, I haven't even gotten through half of the mass killings in the last ten years. The dead pour down like rain.

Two tourists are watching me, smiling. I think they might ask me to take their picture, I prepare myself to fulfill their request, but they unfold a two-meter long metallic pole and place their phone on the end. Can't see the forest for the trees. At this rate it's not hard to deduce that the massacres are going to accumulate to such an extent that I'll have to choose only a selection in the hope of getting through more than twelve months. It'll be easy enough, I'll just pick the massacres and attacks with the highest death tolls. I'll also start reciting them from highest to lowest, not in chronological order anymore: from the killings with the highest death tolls to the ones with the lowest—knowing full well I'll only be reciting the most lethal killings since the start of the millennium, and that's not even including genocides, war crimes, and crimes against humanity (they each have their own list).

And so I'll recite death tolls in the hundred thousands, and then the thousands, and then the hundreds— there won't be time for the dozens. That's how we do things, though, isn't it?—we hold onto the most deadly, most spectacular events, the ones that are the most significant in terms of numbers, then we throw away the rest. It's a sad and arbitrary way to sort through names and fates.

I often think about what my grandparents would say at the table when I'd go have lunch with them on Wednesdays. They'd say *Ava, count yourself lucky, you've never known war.* It makes me laugh now. If my grandparents had known the contents of the lists I recite to myself around the stadium, just from 2008 to the present day, they'd be sick.

I've only got a hundred meters or so left before I arrive at work: I pick up the pace. I pass by the Cartier store; the shutter is lowered. The jewelry is not yet in the display. Two young women clean the large storefront with cloths that they dip into a blue bucket; they're wearing latex gloves and white work shirts; I catch snippets of Spanish spoken in a South-American accent.

I recognize that accent, it's Colombian. Most of the stores aren't open yet except Quick and McDonald's (they open every day at 7 AM). Sometimes I stop and buy a coffee, drinking it as I walk out of a paper cup: the taste doesn't matter much to me. This morning, however, I didn't get a coffee. There's a lingering nervousness. I don't want to amplify it.

Twenty meters farther along, plastered on the window of the Mercedes store is the slogan: NOTHING BUT THE BEST. I appreciate the ambitiousness of the phrase, I've been seeing it every morning for three weeks, along with the luxurious Formula 1 car displayed on a turning platform in the center of the store. Four people have already been ensnared by the car, standing with their hands glued to the windowpane. They seem moved by its beauty—how could you not be, sometimes I, too, stop for a few seconds, morning or night, to admire the race car. But this morning I'm almost late for work; I say "work" but I still hardly believe it, I have trouble believing that I work, that I've become a person with a salary, given that only a year ago I wasn't doing anything but studying, which is to say, loading up on knowledge *for free*. Then I fell into the working world, the world of those who get out of bed in the morning to earn money—a configuration that still feels strange to me, though I know I have to get used to it.

I've gotten to know more or less all the stores on the Champs-Élysées: my lunch breaks have allowed me to explore the environment around my place of work—an absolutely atypical one, might I add. Formula 1 cars in display windows, the official Paris Saint-Germain team store, cinemas, pizzerias, fast food places, and souvenir stores. Luxury and poverty. I've never been able to read while eating, so I settle for strolling down the street, looking for details that might have escaped me. I pass by the storefront of Hugo Boss, and like every time, I think furtively of the Second World War and the Waffen-SS: soldiers in the Waffen-SS wore uniforms specially made by Hugo Boss. Every morning I pass by the store and every morning I can't help but think of the courage it must take to affirm the dignity of a brand after such a dark past.

When I got to the Nike store, I told myself I needed a new pair of shoes. The display window is at least ten meters tall; an orange and yellow neon slogan written across the glass proclaims: INNOVATION FOR A BET- TER LIFE (I translated it since this slogan, like so many others, is in English—it doesn't bug me). Not that I really need a new pair, but the shoes I'm wearing these days are starting to bore me. For four straight weeks I've been wearing them nearly every day. I'm convinced that a new pair would do me good: sometimes spending money can actually be a healthy thing. And what's more, my current shoes are gray and lately gray has been on its way out. It doesn't matter that I don't know if I'm right or wrong—what's the worst that could come from buying a new pair? It's the equivalent of six or seven little paperbacks. A group of soldiers on patrol head toward me. My throat tightens again. I try not to stare at their guns, but I can't help it: my gaze is irresistibly drawn by their weapons of war. To be honest, I've thought about enlisting in the army. After the first wave of attacks, I told myself maybe the army was the answer. I still think about it. To leave, learn a new discipline, learn to overcome my fears—do something with my life. The opportunity to get paid to handle weapons and work out seems worthy of some consideration. Also, I'm not totally indifferent to the idea of holding an assault rifle in my hands. When you're armed, people listen to you, they take you seriously—they finally let you finish your sentences. People don't often let me finish my sentences. I don't know if it's because I'm a girl or because I'm young. Maybe I'm just not speaking loud enough.

It's true that there's one fear holding me back: the fear of killing. I could probably still convince myself that killing isn't such a big deal: it's a matter of adapting. It seems like what they say to new recruits is *the first day is the hardest.* After that, killing becomes routine. It's no more difficult than eating or tending to your basic needs. There's also the fact that I've been touching weapons since my childhood—plastic weapons, to be sure. I massacred zombies with the help of little blue and pink pistols inside the dark arcades of my childhood city, while my whole family (including my sister) was at the beach, building sand castles and playing volleyball. Yes, I have a sister. Her name is Etty; she's two years younger than me, with brown eyes and curly, copper-colored hair. I've always hated the ocean's sand and salt, but my sister adored it. I preferred killing on-screen zombies to lying in the sun. How many hours did I spend glued to the screen, exterminating, exterminating until I felt my thirst become the only obstacle to five more hours of virtual killing? When I shot them, the creatures burst into glittering specks. Imagine my surprise the other night when I heard the testimony of a victim of November 13th say she thought the detonation of the suicide bomber had released a bunch of glitter! She naively believed it was real glitter before realizing it was actually bits of brain speckling her feet and pants. Sorry, but if it had been me, I'd have immediately realized that the suicide bomber had just activated their belt, and that the glittery stuff was nothing other than their whole being, blown into minuscule bits of flesh. Apparently video games did actually prepare me well for real life. God knows I couldn't have imagined ever needing to know such lugubrious things . . . How many times did my grandparents tell me I'd never have to endure what they endured: the violence, the torture, the terror, and the madness of extermination? Looks like they were wrong.

An enormous shadow enters my field of vision: the face of Zlatan Ibrahimovic stretches across the entire length of the Paris Saint-Germain shop window. Across his herculean torso a slogan is written: SPEED, REINVENTED. I need to get a jersey for my sister. I've also omitted a detail: my sister is blind—completely blind. I've promised her so many times to get her a soccer jersey, but I keep forgetting. I don't have any particular affection for PSG, and maybe that's why my mind has concocted a kind of block around this gift. I've been tempted to buy her a jersey from a different team—I was thinking of Boca Juniors—but while my sister might be blind, she is not easily fooled. I'd even say she's more gifted than me when it comes to colors. My sister doesn't see colors, she feels them. Etty knows very well that the PSG colors are blue and red—she remembers the blue and red as she saw them before her *accident*—and I know if I gave her a jersey in any other color, she'd know instantly. I've already asked her numerous times how she does it, how she's able to feel colors, but she can't answer. She settles for telling me that she just knows, and that's all there is to it. But I have to confess, it bugs me, I feel like she's been gifted with a power I don't have—a supernatural power. Maybe she's lying, maybe her brain does perceive visual stimuli when faced with blue or red. But that's not what the doctors say, the ones who look after her eyes. They say that her blindness is total, that in her eyes it is *black as night*.

I pass another group of soldiers. There are six of them. Their gaits are identical: slow, steady steps; their expressions weary. A shameful, unmentionable part of me wants to greet them and thank them for what they do. But something holds me back. It must be said that my mother feared her own country's soldiers: it's likely I inherited that fear.

Don't let the past destroy you

I look up. Thick, swollen clouds of clay-colored gray spread across the sky. I walk past the Disney store. A homeless person is drinking a bottle of red wine at the foot of the shop window, in which two giant figurines glitter—life-size *Stars Wars* stormtroopers. I take a look at my watch: it's 8:44 AM. That man is brave. Whenever I come across a homeless person, I instantly adjust my trajectory: a few centimeters, no more, but I still shift my path slightly. It's not a voluntary thing. It's a reflex. The figurines are carrying weapons similar to the assault rifles I just passed in the street, either AR-15 or M16 (I've done my research): *the semi-automatic rifle used in Sunday's mass shooting costs $759.99 (around 675 euros) and can be legally obtained in the United States in less than seven minutes. It is a weapon designed to kill with maximum ease and efficiency.* To my right, perpendicular to the homeless person, a bank towers sumptuously across the street like a palace. It reminds me that the man who killed Trayvon Martin sold the murder weapon for two hundred and fifty thousand dollars. A good business decision, then. Trayvon Martin's face surfaces in my memory. I think of him often. I'm not exactly sure why—why him and not someone else? If Trayvon Martin hadn't been murdered, I wouldn't know his name or his face; I would never have entered his life, and he would never have entered mine. But Trayvon Martin was murdered. I wonder who bought the gun, who went out and spent two hundred and fifty thousand dollars on an artifact of such injustice.

You got me

Trayvon Martin was shot like a dog in the street, but he didn't succumb to hatred—not even for a moment. All he said to his murderer was: *you got me.* No insult, no reproach. The last words of Trayvon Martin, just after the bullet punctured his lung, were words of absolute clarity. He had the nobility to accept defeat, to accept that he'd been had.

In the last words of Trayvon Martin, I don't hear the singular, but rather the plural: *you got me—all of you, you got me.* And again: *you've all killed me.*

Killed by a violent, racist man.
By a violent, racist system.
By a violent, racist country.
By a violent, racist world.

*

I'll be at work in a moment. I start by modifying my state of mind. As soon as I step through the doors of the store, I'm no longer entirely myself. I smother my affectations, especially those tinged with melancholy. As a general rule, I succeed relatively well at hiding those states of mind. People prefer when you aren't sad, people prefer when you're a ray of sunshine. And how can I argue with them? I run away from everything that threatens to collapse. My reflections are interrupted by a notification from the *New York Times*: it announces a killing that occurred in Los Angeles at 11:00 PM local time, so about sixty minutes ago. While many Americans are already sleeping, our day has just begun. That's the advantage of time zones: it's always rush hour somewhere in the world. That way, no matter where you are, there's always enough people up and about to consume the content as the media report live on any tragedies underway. The news sources are never alone—whether an attack occurs at 3:00 AM, 8:00 AM, at twelve noon or at 6 PM can affect the number of viewers on a national level, but on the international scale, it makes no real impact. Americans are sleeping right now, but don't worry: we're here to replace them, we're there to follow the updates about events on social media; the news dispatches need not be interrupted, nor the live streams or the breaking news segments.

*

I didn't say how afraid I felt this morning on the metro: I tried my best to hide it, to create an illusion. When I get into a subway car, a fleeting, systematic fear grips me—the fear of a bomb or of a belt lined with explosives, hidden in a bag or under a jacket. Any face with too dark or nervous an expression, any movement out of the ordinary: I see red. Any duffel bag or gym bag, a sideways glance, particularly baggy clothing: I just see red.

So daily, the trap of paranoia is set for us. I try to sidestep it, but fear is insistent, it is incarnated in questions as trivial as they are pathetic—should I change compartments, not change compartments, should I just get off now, because he or she is acting weird, at the risk of being wrong or of wasting ten minutes of my day, yes, should I get out now, should I get out and try to save my own skin and not die ravaged by dirty old nails packed into a belt (I still have so much to accomplish) . . . These are the questions that I have to avoid asking myself every day, every time I see a bag or a suitcase left unattended under a seat or on the platform.

I've never talked about this fear with my parents. I don't want to worry them. I can't help but think they'd find me a bit ridiculous, me, who's never known war and who has everything the average Westerner could ever hope for: a roof over my head, a job, a phone, and a laptop swapped out for the newest model every two or three years, a gaming console, a ton of books to read and reread, freedom of movement in a country where women can vote, a country with universal suffrage, where the death penalty has been abolished, where there are no dictators in power, no bloody purges. What could I have to complain about; why could I possibly feel this sick?

End of all innocence

It's true that I'm exaggerating. Statistically, I'm one thousand times more likely to die in a car accident or of heart disease than a terrorist attack. So why this anxiety? *That which is truly irrational, and for which there is no explanation, is not evil—on the contrary, it is goodness.* It took me a while to understand this quote: not intellectually, but to understand it in my bones. I then had to resign myself to the obvious: I believe perfectly in its meaning. I'd even go so far as to call the man who wrote it a bastard. I say to myself: what a bastard, he saw it all so clearly. It's no longer possible to avoid this truth, to circumvent it, everything is made in such a way that this sentence rules the world, everything is made (especially these days) in such a way that reality reveals itself to us as having been constructed on a bedrock of evil and not goodness, so that horror, not beauty, is our world's point of reference. I want to believe the complete opposite, I want to believe that this sentence is fundamentally wrong, but the facts contradict me. Everywhere, the numbers and their cold precision make a liar out of me.

Only twenty meters to go. I see my employer's logo (a white apple with a bite taken out of it). On the street, a young woman is begging. She must be about my age. Her child is next to her, kneeling, his head resting tenderly on his mother's right shoulder. He's wearing tiny red Adidas sneakers. His face is singularly beautiful, his skin olive, his hair black, and eyes dark. A cat on a leash is sleeping deeply at their feet next to a cardboard sign that says FOR FOOD in black marker, spelled out in thick but shaky capital letters. A plastic cup sits next to the sign, and the mother regularly empties it to make it seem as though people have given nothing (according to my observations, the method is tried and true).

I know these panhandlers; they're out here Mondays, Thursdays and Saturdays. Tuesdays and Fridays I pass them further up the street, across from the Quick. Her husband panhandles on Place de la Concorde. I know they're married because they pass the child back and forth—one day he's with her, the next with him. I don't yet understand why they beg with their child. I don't know if it's because there isn't anyone to watch him, or if it's to pull on the heartstrings of passersby and make more money. Like most people, I don't ever give them money. In reality, I'd rather not see them: I'd like them to disappear. Not only are they not disappearing, they're proliferating. In the metro, on the platforms, on the boulevards and streets, families pick a spot and settle there— entire families living on the street, sharing their mattress. What I've just said unsettles you. I know. It disturbs me just as much as it does you (I'm not quite as cynical as you'd like to believe), but either I share everything or I start to lie. I'm happy lying to others, but with you, it's more complicated. Let's just say that I have nothing to gain from lying to you. I'd even say I have everything to lose.

And since I've just affirmed I'm not lying to you, I'm going to confess something: I'm not going to work, for the simple reason that exactly three weeks ago I lost my job. I keep getting up at seven in the morning, taking the metro here and just spending the day outside. I do it to keep myself afloat, because I know myself: if I don't keep forcing myself to get up in the morning and leave the house, if I don't keep pretending I have a job, my entire existence will fall apart.

3

One day, you'll close your eyes.
DZHOKHAR TSARNAEV, nineteen

I can't stop going over my last day in my head. I remember the exact time I arrived at the store. As I passed through the doors, I checked my watch: it was 8:32 AM. I greeted the security guard and then I made a beeline for the staff room. Baptiste, the guy in charge of the accessories department (batteries, chargers, earbuds, headphones, and cases), was there, leaning against his locker, eyes riveted on his phone, shoulders hunched, and thumbs glued to the screen. He lifted his head and said: *hey*. I didn't answer. I settled for just smiling—a primal smile, almost animalistic in its neutrality. I stopped by my locker, I unlocked it—it was protected by a four number combination, I chose the number *2001*—then I opened it. My locker contained a bit of everything: a copy of the Bible, a box of Smarties, a photo of James Joyce playing guitar, a printed-out screenshot of the last SpaceX shuttle launch, a spare blue T-shirt stamped with the company logo, tennis balls (I sometimes have doubles on Wednesday nights), two copies of *National Geographic* (I don't know how those got in there), an aluminum selfie stick, a Yankees hat, and an old copy of Nerval's *Filles du feu* bought from a bookseller on the Grands-Augustins quay and left to rot there. As I was saying: I opened my locker and I stuffed my wallet and cellphone inside—I never kept my phone on me during work hours, out of fear of being unable to resist the temptation to send and respond to personal messages (something that's naturally prohibited)—careful to ensure the piles of objects didn't collapse. I shut the locker door. Baptiste remained in the same position, the bags under his eyes shining, incandescent as pearls, in the light of his phone screen. Without taking his eyes off the screen, he told me our manager was calling a meeting around 9:00 AM to announce the sales numbers from the last quarter. It was 8:40 AM. I had some time before the meeting. I unlocked my locker for the second time. I took out my phone. I turned off airplane mode and then I opened my social media app of choice. A video of a decapitation had just appeared on my news feed, put online by someone I'd never met. I turned the sound down and I watched the video of the man being decapitated in the middle of the desert. He seemed young, no more than twenty-five, he was wearing an orange tunic, and had a shaved head. The face of his executioner was hidden beneath a black hood, only his thick-bladed knife was visible. While I watched the video, Baptiste started telling me about how, by saving half of his pay for thirty-six months and taking out a loan at 3 percent, he'd be able to buy the car of his dreams (a self-driving Tesla). I said something encouraging. You should go after your dreams, whatever they might be. To buy a self-driving car. To build a space shuttle. Travel around the world. Fall madly in love. Get a promotion. All I know is: you have to go for it.

I don't know what my dream is

My coworker was a fanatic. Technology was nothing more or less than his *raison d'être*: "The destiny of humanity," as he said. He was the complete opposite of the store manager, our superior in the hierarchy, who was a pure rationalist. He remained within the perimeter of his tasks, making sure to never step beyond them, executing the orders that came from the United States with solicitousness and precision, but never excessive devotion. In twelve months, I'd never heard our manager speak about a long term vision for the company: he simply didn't have one, just as he showed no interest in the incendiary debates between Baptiste and some of our other coworkers that went on during the lunch break. Most recently, our topic of discussion had been the end of the world. Baptiste had gone over the three major risks, already being projected and discussed in the boardrooms of Silicon Valley: first, the end of the world brought about by a contagious and lethal virus propagated by terrorist forces; second, the end of the world brought on by a rebelling artificial intelligence which chooses to turn on its creator and destroy humanity; third, and the most likely scenario, a nuclear world war, wherein humanity exterminates itself. Baptiste didn't forget to praise certain millionaires who've stockpiled weapons, gold, antibiotics, gas masks from the Israeli military, not to mention purchased bunkers and large plots of land in Big Sur, where they'll take refuge when the time comes. No, to our boss, ideology was first and foremost logistical and administrative: he was neither a mystic nor a prophet, which leads me to believe that, in this way, he was perfectly suited to his work: managing a store and a team with rigor and precision, without letting himself be overwhelmed by motivations of a spiritual order.

I'm getting off track. Anyway: I turned off my phone. I buried it in my locker. I closed the door and waited, standing in front of it for fifteen minutes. At 9:00 AM, an hour before the opening of the store, the manager gathered all the morning employees in a circle: six salespeople (four on the ground floor, two upstairs), three technicians from customer service, two stockroom employees (including me), and the security guard. The sales numbers from the last quarter were explosive: we'd set an unprecedented record for the Ile-de-France region. I was a little surprised, having heard the day before on TV that our country's economic growth had been undergoing an accelerated decline for the past few months. Then I remembered an article that claimed massive acts of violence create a collective anguish and anxiety conducive to short term bursts of economic growth as households seek consolation. These sales records confirm the theory that the more deaths there are, the more revenues are likely to increase.

Before ending the meeting, our manager reminded us that the authorities had planned a moment of silence for the nation to pay respect to the victims (I can't deal with that word) of the previous day's attack. We were asked to pause all activity between 11:59 AM and noon.

During my trial period, which lasted two months, my work essentially consisted of arranging and rearranging products (computers, phones, and tablets) along the long wooden tables on the ground floor, so that they were all aligned with one another. If certain products were damaged or if the custodial staff had neglected to clean them,

I'd dust them myself with the help of a little gray Lycra cloth that I sprayed with a blue liquid (generally used to clean windows). Then I repositioned the computers, tablets, and phones: first the largest screens, then the smaller ones: I traced an imaginary line and laid each product down along it so that they were positioned symmetrically. The manager's watchword was *purity*: every morning he repeated: *everything has to be pure.* I didn't have any direct contact with customers, but I observed them. The thing that struck me most was how few conflicts and meltdowns there were amongst the clientele. Having briefly worked in a fast food restaurant and then in a clothing store, that struck me as remarkable: the customers respected this place. Its beauty, its cleanliness, its orderliness elicited a quasi-religious sentiment. Occasionally, of course, an outlier would decide to work something out on a display model—they'd fulfill our wreckage quota. But nothing crazy. The person responsible would be quickly overwhelmed by the security personnel, no drama, no violence. The fit of rage was neutralized according to a perfectly mundane protocol, so well executed that the rare acts of revolt, taking place in the middle of customer comings and goings, passed unnoticed, and were reduced to nothingness as quickly as they had begun.

Once the trial period was over, I was assigned to a position responsible for the reserves in the stockroom. My taste for silence, solitude, order and structure played an undeniable role in my being given the position in the store basement. In reality, it's a rare thing to be able to endure more than a half an hour down there. But I did six to eight hours a day. Strangely, in that locked basement, I felt at ease, I'd even say: in my element.

The stockroom was an enormous rectangular space; if I had to describe its atmosphere, I'd say it felt like an airport chapel—a contemplative space surrounded by endless movement, a place where the sacred is made present, not through any memory contained in the walls, but rather by the place's own virtual symbolism. In the center of the room stood a huge square block of gray concrete, fitted with sliding panels that could be manipulated with the help of round, stainless-steel grips. From far away, it might have been mistaken for a library. Inside, it was a downright labyrinth of rows and shelves of devices that would be sold in the next seventy-two hours. Deliveries took place twice a week, on Tuesday and Thursday—that's to say, as far as I was concerned, once a week (Thursday was my day off). Only three people had the access code to open the stockroom: the store manager and the two employees working in there. The code was changed twice a week. The cleaners who took care of the basement weren't the same ones who worked the first floor: to have access to this room, you needed special authorization—it was a world within a world.

I never met the stockroom cleaners; they must have worked at night or early dawn. Sometimes, around 8:00 AM, the smell of lilac and bleach still greeted whoever opened the metal door. That smell was the only trace of their presence, and that's why I liked it.

So I managed the flow: I made inventories of everything that arrived in the stockroom and everything that went up to the store; I scanned the series numbers of the products, then I verified if those series numbers corresponded to the merchandise received, as well as to the quantities indicated on the bills of lading. Once those verifications were taken care of, my coworker and I (his name was Kévin, we spoke rarely) began putting away the new merchandise in the stockroom under the watchful gaze of the security cameras.

The working conditions were difficult for me, but the issue wasn't anything physical: it was nervous. Essentially, I was only interacting with machines, and those machines did everything their own way: submission can be a challenging ordeal for the human being that I am. To keep track of the merchandise stock levels, for example, I used a software program that militantly set out to correct every hint of logical discrepancy: to this program, there was only one way to act, and if I didn't follow the method with complete and scrupulous obedience, it would stonewall me.

I had no choice but to obey.

I eventually began to question my own usefulness. My coworker was encountering the same problem: the software carried on very well without us. The tiredness came not so much from an experience of conflict, but more from the absence of it: there was no possible dialogue, the very concept of listening was unknown to the program. What's more, it had the capacity to automatically learn from its mistakes: it autocorrected. In twelve months, I watched it grow, gain strength, while we became weaker and weaker.

*

At 11:30 AM, I took my break (besides the thirty-minute lunch break, we were entitled to one ten-minute break in the morning and one in the afternoon). I left the warehouse and headed into the staff room. I unlocked my locker, opened the door and took out my phone. I checked to see if the number of recorded deaths from last night's attack had increased (two more had been added). On the website of one of France's three main daily news outlets, a chart entitled "Human Toll" had just been posted: on the left, fifteen little purple squares represented the *dead children*, and eighty-two light red squares represented the *dead adults*; in the center, orange squares represented the wounded *on life support* and yellow squares those *in critical condition;* finally, toward the right section of the graph, the wounded who were *expected to make a full recovery* made up nearly a hundred blue squares. I didn't bother to count them all, there were too many. No names, only numbers.

At 11:50 AM, I left the staffroom and made my way to the section that carried silicone cases. I set my mind to imagining a slaughter in this store. I saw the bits of brain lying on the beautiful white, black and pearly gray objects, the bodies slumped over tables and on the ground, on the sparkling floor that's cleaned every morning. And that morning, like every other, as I walked through the large glass doors and greeted the security guard, I thought: he doesn't even have a gun, which means he's useless.

Zero risk doesn't exist

Not a day went by that I didn't imagine the worst. During my breaks, I sometimes gave my paranoia free rein: I'd look at each of the clients in turn and I'd imagine each of them being killed execution style in front of the big glass staircase. To pass the time, I entertained myself by classifying the faces: those who were brave by nature, those who were brave out of self-interest, and the cowards—I knew that out of a sample of a hundred customers, there were probably sixty cowards, thirty who were brave for their own sake, and ten who were brave by nature.

If one or more people had burst violently into the store, I'd have locked myself in the warehouse, and then into the cube containing the merchandise, hoping to survive long enough for law enforcement to arrive. No point in playing hero. What's more, we never had any training: if an attack had happened, we wouldn't have been prepared. According to what I've learned from watching surveillance footage, the explosion of a bomb in a public place always produces the same effect: in an instant, human beings become wild animals; they run in every direction, chaotically, to get as far as possible from the point of impact. The dispersal of the bodies is like a firework show, or a flower blooming in time-lapse. I remain perplexed by the phenomenon: there is a beauty to it (I'm ashamed to say), this geography of horror.

Two minutes before noon, I anticipated the moment of silence and closed my eyes. I've been through dozens of minutes of silence. I remember my first one; it was in honor of the victims of September 11th, we were in class and all the students watched each other, lips closed, for sixty-seconds. That's the major problem with moments of silence: no one knows what to do when nobody is speaking. All things considered, I was a little sad— at least I tried to be. I thought about the people who died in the towers; the people who threw themselves into the void; the children who saw their mothers or fathers commit suicide live on television, jumping from the ninetieth floor, preferring to die from a skull shattered on pavement than suffocation.

But it wasn't on September 11th that I first experienced the shock of terror: I was still too young. The first time was the 18th and 19th of April, 2013, the day of the manhunt for Dzhokhar Tsarnaev. I memorized this summary by heart from Wikipedia: *On the night of April 18th, a shootout occurred on MIT campus that would take the life of a university police officer. The two brothers hijacked a car. Its driver was taken hostage and managed to escape while they were stopped at a gas station. The portable phone that the hostage had left in the car made it possible to locate the terrorists. A chase ensued during the night in Watertown, followed by a shootout, in the course of which fifteen police officers were wounded and one of the suspects was taken into custody. That suspect died shortly thereafter of his wounds—it was Tamerlan Tsarnaev, twenty-six years old (born October 21, 1986). The other individual, his nineteen-year-old brother, Dzhokhar Tsarnaev (born July 22, 1993), the second suspect in the attacks, managed to flee, and was considered to be armed and dangerous. Nine thousand armed officers patrolled Boston, which had become a ghost town, as well as its environs: citizens were encouraged not to go to work, to return home and barricade their houses. Watertown in particular was searched house by house. Dzhokhar Tsarnaev, wounded, was found by a resident under a tarp covering his boat once the curfew had been lifted. Dzhokhar Tsarnaev was finally arrested by the authorities at 8:45 PM local time after a last burst of gunfire during which he was again wounded. According to an official source, he was in fact unarmed and carried no explosives at the time of his arrest.*

I followed the manhunt for the terrorist all day. Meaning I spent more than twelve hours in front of the TV. Out of a combination of emotion and exhaustion, the reporters ended up calling Dzhokhar Tsarnaev by his first name. This was the first step toward his transformation into a hero. The police, the military, the secret service—hundreds of them were required to hunt down a boy two years younger than me.

After the night of April 19th, 2013, I no longer looked at the world the same way.

Terrorism was everywhere, buried like a seed inside every body. The very foundations of my innocence had just been threatened. Every person I saw, every child, maybe him, maybe her, was one day, potentially, going to set off a bomb. The virus of terror was omnipresent. I don't get sad anymore during moments of silence. I've even learned how to dispel my own unease. I've created a protocol: I close my eyes and try to remember the dream I had the night before. This method is effective in passing the time, I'd even say that while using it, I don't notice the minute pass. Something I also like to do, if I'm at home, is turn on the radio right at noon: there's nothing on air, just silence. Silence on the radio is an evolved form of perfection: you can't surprise a listener more than by ceasing all speech.

I stopped reflecting during these moments a long time ago. That day, during the moment of silence, I reopened my eyelids again after a couple of seconds and stared at a screensaver in my field of vision. We all respected the moment of silence, of course, with the exception of a tourist who was on the phone, but you can't fault him for it, he probably didn't know what was going on—no one took offense. And anyway, I call it a minute but it was more like fifty seconds: it's impossible to have an actual minute of silence. Toward the final third, you feel people start to lose their focus and interest.

I could have done something else during that minute, been productive, but I had to sacrifice it to the victims instead, which means also to the murderers. I think of the insane amount of time a country loses administratively because of violence. The moments of silence are only a tiny part of all that lost time; there are hours, days, nights lost spent following the news, trying to find out the exact number of dead, the names of the terrorists, the names of the victims—not to mention the amount of time lost to feeding fear.

At 5:10 PM, my fate was sealed. I was in the stockroom with only twenty minutes of work left. I was struggling with the management software that keeps track of the serial numbers, it wouldn't stop crashing, something that generally happened after a long day of work. On my right, sitting on a stool, my coworker was playing Tetris on his phone. My eyes bounced between his screen and my own, dizzied by the movement of continuously falling squares. Suddenly, I heard footsteps on the stairs. The door opened. It was the store manager. My coworker hastily shut off his phone screen. The squares disappeared. He put his phone in his pocket. The manager came over to us. He was wearing a black turtleneck. He had a neutral look on his face. He took me aside and said, smiling: "Ava, we're going to have to let you go." Then, he added: "Your performance is good, but you don't have the faith. I don't feel like you're one of us."

II

To have been made human without the possibility
of being human—that is the cruelest punishment of all.
DYLAN KLEBOLD, seventeen

I wanted to experience life to the extreme.
I found myself in hell.
ANONYMOUS RADICALIZED YOUTH, nineteen

The Holocaust is not over.
TIMOTHY SNYDER

1

I wandered around Paris all morning. My eyes burned and stung. As the hours passed, my tiredness grew. Reality became a delirious, opaque material, slowly extracting itself from my body. The sound of the city was unrelenting, harsh, and painful. Horns, Sirens, the rush of air from exhaust pipes—together they constituted the intensity of a metropolis contaminated by machines. I walked slowly, aimlessly. Everyone else passed right by me. I lingered in the squares. My shoes got covered in dust. I hate dust: it reminds me of ashes. I went to the Louvre, I thought about going in but I was afraid that a young nihilist might set off a bomb there. I need to stop with all that. I'm only feeding fear, which is to say, death, which is to say hatred.

Give life, not death

I thought about my CV every five minutes like clockwork. More specifically, I thought: it needs to be expanded and embellished. This is a permanent, subterranean anxiety, an administrative task that never ceases to catch up with me, try as I might to bury it each morning. I have to redo my CV, make it more appealing, but also more compact and digestible—that's how I'll find work. It's not acceptable to have such a hard time finding a job at my age (barely a quarter of a century), even just a temporary one. I should highlight my serious commitment to sports and my mastery of English. Anyway . . .

I checked my phone compulsively as I walked, jumping between different social media apps and news articles, over and over—all to hold my ennui at bay. The regularity, the diversity and the abundance of information never ceases to move me: in four minutes, I learned that three hundred infants died in the Mediterranean sea in the span of one hundred and eighty days; that liquid water had been found on Mars; that a bombing in Ankara caused twenty-eight deaths; that a terrorist attack in Burkina Faso killed twenty-nine people ("the assailants looked like children"); that growth in China is declining; that the space robot Philae sent a final data set before "falling into a coma"; that holding someone's gaze for 3.2 second "changes everything"; that women can't go to sports stadiums any more in Iran; that fifty Shiites were killed near Damascus; that a man convicted of homosexuality in Deir Ez-Zor had been thrown from a rooftop; that ten terrorist plots have been thwarted in

France in the last twenty-four months ("we're walking on eggshells," declared the Minister of the Interior); that only twelve percent of terrorist recruits want to die as martyrs; that the migrant crisis represents the most important migration of human populations in Europe since the Second World War; that the museum at Auschwitz finds itself overwhelmed by mass tourism, and—to me, the loveliest journalistic surprise of the last twenty-four hours, found randomly thanks to the involuntary movement of my thumb across the touch screen while I scrolled down the homepage of *Le Monde*—the discovery in Kenya of the oldest battle in human history: "They remained there. No one came to gather their bodies. They lay scattered amongst the dunes, some stretched out along the long bank of sand and fine gravel, or on the little hills, others even floating in the lagoon. There were just about thirty of them, men, women (one of whom was pregnant), and several children, all dead in battle or simply massacred. One man had a broken knee, and an arrowhead embedded in his skull. Another had been struck in the temple and the neck. There was one woman with her hands broken and her forehead bashed in ... The list of injuries is long and morbid, compiled painstakingly by an international team of archaeologists and anthropologists long after the site's discovery at Nataruk in 2012 by a Kenyan assistant. It's located west of Lake Turkana, in

Kenya, on the edge of an ancient little lagoon. Thanks to the shells lying around the skeletons, archaeologists were able to estimate the time period during which the deceased lived: around ten thousand years ago." Sorry for all the details. I feel like it's important to share the news: after all, what's a news dispatch if not firstly an encounter? It can change a life. Or, just as easily, disappear. In my case, I generally only ever retain one hundredth or even one thousandth of all the information I encounter, just like I only retain the memory of one face out of a hundred or a thousand . . . That doesn't change my daily need to devour the news or meet the gaze of strangers.

It's also probably the reason my phone is my everyday ally: I can't stand being alone—I'm always waiting to be changed by an encounter.

*

Around 11:00 AM, I wound up on boulevard Voltaire. I mean to say I made it so, I made it so that I'd end up there—out of obsession, voyeurism, inertia (I don't know which of the many possible causes claims this victory). I walked to number fifty. The entrance to the concert hall was no longer hidden by a tarp. It had been renovated. The eight letters on the wall, once black on a white background, had now become red: blood red.

I was right at the epicenter of the killing. My feet were touching the same sidewalk the murderers themselves walked along. Since November, every time I find myself in front of this hall, I feel a mixture of terror and morbid fascination: I see that dark night all over again; the night everything changed. I even relive the race that went on to capture it, photograph it. Hurried breaking news segments. The bodies dragged into the adjacent street. The father screaming in the Amelot laneway, trying to find his son: OSCAR, OSCAR! The wounded and the hostages evacuated from the scene of the crime, some with their hands in the air. A potential terrorist among the victims. The suspicion. The uncertainty. The pain of the wounded. The pain of the families. The torture of waiting. The flashing police car lights reflected on the stone of the buildings. The City of Light under siege. The fear. The solidarity. The blood in the concert hall and in the courtyards of apartment buildings. The neighbors' doors opening. The blood of unknown young people on carpets in nearby apartments. Their blood on the sofa. Inert bodies piled in the mosh pit. The young man who'd just been slain. The young woman who'd just been slain. The lives being extinguished at random. Large scale human sacrifice. Right in the middle of the nation's capital. The smell of guts from the pit. The ring of victims' cell phones going unanswered. Answering machines full of messages. Abandoned shoes, mismatched and lying on the asphalt all around where I'm now standing. The pregnant woman, so close to falling into the abyss but saved by a heroic hand. The silence in my apartment. The messages I received. My parents' anxiety. The courage of the rescue team. The solitude. The shock. The bravery. The cowardice.

And the sleepless night that followed. The streets— deserted but for a few faces, dazed and stupefied by the echoes of such an evening of violence. The fog. The milky sky. The total silence. The empty city squares. The children kept home. The smell of mourning. The wounded the dead the enemies. All losers—only loss.

In front of this place, now completely renovated (hellish amnesia), I said this to myself, all of a sudden, I swore it like a promise to be kept until the end of my days: you are not doomed to dwell on death. You are not destined to destruction. You are not condemned to be fascinated by blood, by bombs, by weapons—by evil in all of its incarnations. And I heard that phrase I loved so much: *what is truly irrational, and for which there is no explanation, is not evil—on the contrary, it is goodness.* Stop concentrating on violence and death. Work to defend beauty. Simple. The thing that doesn't fascinate. In the same way that goodness does not fascinate. In the same way that peace does not fascinate.

You aren't screwed no you are not a lost cause

I remembered the moment I started collecting the terrorists' faces and sticking them on the wall of my bedroom, as if they were heroes. There's no point in hiding it—sometimes I do get them mixed up: I remember the face of one of the three terrorists and think he's one of the victims (I use the word *victim* repeatedly, I haven't found anything better). It must be said that their appearance doesn't help much: they have the same juvenile features; the same smile; the same innocent eyes as their prey. Twenty-three years old, twenty-eight, twenty-nine. And then I have to admit it—in spite of myself, I am linked to them, and they to me. By age, of course. But that's not all. Two months ago, I got a brochure in the mail about measures to protect against the risk of radicalization, with diagrams, charts, and percentages. It grouped behaviors into four categories: insignificant behaviors (green light), concerning behaviors (yellow light), worrisome behaviors (orange light), alarming behaviors (red light). *Has someone in your life gone through a dramatic change in lifestyle or behavior? Have they begun to isolate themselves? Do they frequently employ a polarizing rhetoric of absolute truth, exhibit paranoia or extreme suspiciousness? Have they suddenly lost interest in their professional or educational pursuits? Do they express support for the use of violence to defend a cause? Do they express a desire to integrate or deepen an existing religious practice, commitment to an identity, or political affiliation? Have*

*they become obsessed with the end of the world or with mes-
sianic discourses? Do they talk about leaving the country?*
When faced with such behaviors, the brochure indicates
four possible reactions: worry, concern, panic, and, as a
last resort, reporting the behaviors to the authorities.
My first instinct was to laugh, for the simple reason that
this brochure was talking about *me*.

At seven years old, I was already into killing. More
precisely: I massacred virtual bodies. In video games,
the more you exterminate, the more chance you'll win.
At thirteen, in junior high, I began to feel excluded.
We were judged on our grades: we became numbers.
In the schoolyard, it was about clothes. Brands gave us
our identities. Pretty or ugly; dateable or undateable. In
French Republic schools there was no point in trying
to talk about religion. Early on, I became obsessed with
leaving, with death and with God. When I was a child
and I'd get up in the middle of the night, I felt God
behind me. It wasn't a nightmare or a fantasy: I'd heard
in a catechism class that God was always behind us, and
I had the misfortune of taking that phrase literally. It
should have reassured me, but in reality, it frightened
me terribly. I felt God lurking behind me, he became a
weight, a threat, and every time I got up in the middle
of the night to go to the bathroom, I looked over my
shoulder, afraid of finding a face, a body or a pair of
hands following me.

Faith was infused into my life by all possible means—everyone wanted me to believe. I needed a rigorousness, a precision; I needed a world. I found that place in books. I think it's fair to say that, in my own way, I *was* radicalized. Without books, maybe I'd have been pulled under, have let myself be ravaged by the fear of failure; by supermarkets and their smell of plastic and their tasteless vegetables; by the formless models devoid of humanity, sold to girls as examples of desirability and eroticism; by video games; by television. And to vengeance, to the desire to take revenge on myself or others—who knows? Maybe one encounter is enough to change everything. I think if at sixteen I'd fallen on a manifesto of hatred instead of a book of poetry, it might have been possible: I might have been turned.

I contemplated the faces of these terrorists insistently. I searched for the evil in their eyes; I wanted to understand evil. Like I told you, I didn't always tend toward violent things—it happened over time, as the world slowly revealed its inner workings, as I left the blind comfort of childhood. It's not entirely my fault. It was the stuff of banal everyday life that pushed me toward horror's embrace. News reports on TV, video games, morbid photographs floating around social media—every day: hundreds of children dead on beaches, vomited out by the sea, or simply murdered on the pure whim of such and such an army, regime or democracy! Wiped off the face of the earth like invasive pests by bombings, shootings, sarin gas—what do I know, there have always been too many options when it comes to murder. I devoured the images, one after another, day after day, month after month, year after year. And little by little, horror became acceptable. Still nauseating. But tolerable. I mean *human*. And that's what must be fought. I remember—that's the hardest thing, the cruelest thing: that we have to keep trying to be shocked by these things.

This morning, in the street, I wanted to throw my phone away: I was hit by the desire to smash it on the sidewalk. To sever the invisible rope around my neck. To renounce objects. Renounce the online world. Leave. Start over. But not by killing, not by massacring, not by spouting hatred. It's not courage that gives us the nerve to kill ourselves in the middle of a crowd or in our own bedroom amongst all our old toys. That's not bravery. It's fear. Fear of death. Fear of love. Fear of joy. That's exactly what threatens us: the fear of being alive.

Forgive me . . . I need to pull myself together. I gave in to anger. But you have to understand—I can't just go on like everything is fine. I want to, but I'm just not capable.

I kept walking, distractedly. On the wall of an elementary school, I noticed a plaque commemorating eleven children who were deported. They're all around Paris. Purple roses, faded and wilting, were stuck to it. Plaques will need to be put up to commemorate the November 13th massacres—made out of marble, to ensure rust won't gnaw away at them. There'll be one for each attack: like there is for each group of children rounded up (eleven thousand little kids deported, if my calculations are correct). We'll lay down an offering of flowers as often as possible. We have to concede that I'm lucky to live in a country that takes charge of maintaining commemorative plaques. That's not to say some aren't neglected: it's simply impossible to keep all of the one thousand plus memorials in good condition, not to mention all those still to come. But repairs will be ensured for the vast majority—we do what we can.

Around noon, I went into a supermarket and bought two cans of pop with aspartame. I drank them standing, right beside the store exit, in front of a big family sitting on their mattresses on the street. They were a little flock, sitting there, the mother on the left, four children in the middle (at a glance, I'd say they were between five and thirteen years old), and the father on the right. For a moment I felt the urge to speak to them, but naturally, I restrained myself—I even regretted that sudden overflowing of humanism. I felt like it should be illegal, me standing there in the face of such poverty.

The idea of chewing food disgusted me. I can't believe we're still chewing: here we are, capable of exploring the solar system; capable of annihilating eighty thousand people with one bomb; but we still have to chew our food to survive. It's about time I started to feed myself exclusively using liquids, like some of my coworkers used to do on our lunch break: a nutrient-complete drinkable solution, five hundred calories per five hundred milliliters: twenty-five grams of protein, twenty-five grams of fat, twenty-five grams of carbohydrates—as economical as can be, and what's more, *you'll never have to think about feeding yourself again* (according to the slogan). It won me over immediately. I almost ordered a whole box before being interrupted at the last moment by a conservative impulse. I'm not worried, though. That too will disappear in the end.

2

It's a little before 6:00 PM, I'm on Avenue de Flandre, sitting at the counter of a bar-tabac on a metal stool with a little round black cushion made of fake leather. The room is narrow and the zinc counter hugs the whole length of it. The built-in pot lights speckle the ceiling, and as for the smell, it would have to be described as a combination of wet dog, musty old coats, and beer. Behind the counter, the guy manning the bar is busy adding grenadine to a glass of milk. The whiteness of the milk is soiled, little by little, by the syrup. *One Parisian death is worth the same as ten thousand deaths elsewhere.* I raise my head. A television hangs from the wall next to the selection of whiskeys. I can make out Marc Trévidic on a TV set. He's wearing a pink polo and a black jacket. The bartender calls out to me: "What can I get for you?"—"Half a pint of Carlsberg." "We don't have any today. It's got to be Kro, Leffe, or Grim." I hesitate. Marc Trévidic repeats

One Parisian death is worth a thousand deaths elsewhere. "Kronenbourg," I answer. Maybe it's a mistake: I rarely drink just a half pint. Usually, it's either two half pints, water, soda, or coffee. By way of explanation, you should know I didn't eat breakfast—that means I have to stick to just one half pint. *The death of one Parisian is worth ten thousand deaths elsewhere.* If I drink two of these beers (a full pint) I'll fall into a gentle drunkenness. I can't get a little drunk without risking melancholy— exactly the thing I'm fighting. And what's more, being drunk before 8:00 PM isn't really socially acceptable, it would be tantamount to admitting my whole life is falling apart, including my sense of discipline. I can't lose that: it's the only thing that I've been able to maintain. *Worth.* Why talk in terms of worth? A death isn't worth anything. History has more than proved that to us.

There isn't just one television here, there are three: the first screen is anchored above the bar, facing my seat; the second is on my left; the third on my right. They're all showing the same channel, which means all the same gestures and faces bloom simultaneously in three places across the room. I saw three Marc Trévidics and heard him speak three times, at infinitesimal intervals (a few hundredths of a second difference): it's true that a livestream is never perfectly 'live,' there's always a tiny time lag between the set to the screen, and then from one screen to another. The bartender tosses a cardboard coaster on the counter, and sets my beer down a few inches from my phone. A drop of liquid splashes onto my screen. That carelessness bothers me. I wipe the surface of the phone with my sleeve. "Wasn't it you that forgot that little book the other day?" he asks me, raising his left eyebrow. I answer, saying it's possible. *The death of one Parisian is worth the deaths of ten thousand others,* if I've understood the logic properly, being a Westerner today means carrying the weight of nine thousand nine hundred and ninety-nine deaths. The bartender disappears under the counter (so I guess I forgot my book here and not on my desk, like I thought for a moment on the metro this morning, which makes sense since I don't remember leaving it on my desk).

I first started coming to this place when I was working in the stockroom. In the evening, after prolonged hours of working with packing materials and screens, I could no longer feel the tips of my fingers: they became basically numb to all sensation. Hot, cold, rough, soft, hard, squishy—I could no longer tell the difference. Sometimes after work, I'd use this place as a kind of decompression chamber. I could come here after a draining day and just be silent, anonymous, lost in the flow of beer and apéritif-drinkers, and seasoned gamblers, too, with their slot machines and their horse races. A non-violent way of navigating my temporary return to the world of humanity.

The bartender reappears. I look into his face. He has a thin nose, slanted eyes, and blackheads on his chin; he's wearing a gray spandex shirt which reflects the light, with the sleeves rolled up. He sets my book down on the counter, next to my phone. "I told myself it had to be you, you've always got your nose in a book," he adds, an ambiguous smile on his lips. A black and white photo of the author gazing into the distance adorns the book cover. His almond-shaped eyes are deep and bright. *Two children had their throats slit in Paris this morning, outside an elementary school, it would appear to be an act of* . . . I raise my eyes to the TV. The manager furrows his brow. He turns toward the screen and raises the volume. I am drawn irresistibly toward it. The faces around me contemplate it with the same twitchy fascination, looking back at it every ten seconds like a kind of hypnosis. Two Parisian children are dead, which matters as much as twenty thousand children elsewhere. Is that possible? Whatever we think, Marc Trévidic could have at least taken the utter incommensurability of death into account . . . So the death of one Parisian child might as well be the death of every child on Earth. I agree with you, this line of reasoning may sound nice, but it doesn't hold up. How about this: the dead must be counted. Counted precisely, and with reference to certain measures. If we don't count them rigorously, keep track, we'll lose all sense of our priorities. And those need to be maintained: the loss of human life is inevitable—true—and better for a bomb to fall on Aleppo than on the French capital (don't bother with any whiny humanitarian speeches, even the United Nations understands the way things work). The UN understands that peace is a posture. They understand who dominates and who submits. The memory of the United Nations building in New York comes back to me. Such magnificent architecture. I don't really know what they do inside, but that doesn't matter: it's a place of unique beauty. There's no need to state the obvious, that Le Corbusier and Niemeyer did an extraordinary job—even more impressive when you consider what they had to work with . . . That magnificent skyscraper was built right on the site of the city's old slaughterhouse. Thousands of cattle and pigs were probably killed there (industrial scale slaughter), and surely turned into hundreds of thousands of units of product. And then one fine day, a new project came along to redeem that blight; and so this sublime temple to humanism was born, with its ambitious height (155 meters tall, I don't know how wide, I looked hard on Google, but to no avail). *According to witnesses, the event unfolded just before 5:30 PM, we don't know yet whether there are other children to be counted among the victims.* No more slaughterhouses. No more blood: say hello to the headquarters of the United Nations. I just said we were done with slaughterhouses and blood, but that's wrong: after all, and proudly so, the United Nations have done nothing else but negotiate with other kinds of slaughterhouses. And it's not the blood of cattle or pigs being spilt, but human blood (spilled at a rate and on a scale on par with the former owners of the property).

From one slaughterhouse comes another

I take another sip of beer. I think of my sister, then of my mother—I think of their grief. I haven't told you this, but today makes six days since my grandmother died. I think about her once or twice an hour. I forget she's dead, then I remember: she keeps dying over and over again. My memory has held onto everything. The softness of the skin on her hands, her hoarse, fragile voice, her laugh, the smell of her dresses. Right now I should be at the other end of the world with my parents and my sister, getting ready for the burial. But instead I stayed here. Out of cowardice. Because it was easier. My sister must be so angry I didn't go with her. The plane, the airport, the hellishness of the transitions, my grandmother's house suddenly empty, the weight of absence, my mother's grief—it was all too much. I can't bear to see my mother in tears.

Someone taps me gently on the shoulder. I turn and a man in a sky-blue shirt asks me in broken French what's going on. His gestures express his unease. He doesn't understand much of what I'm trying to explain to him, but the word "terroriste" still makes his eyes widen. A special news segment has just been announced on the TV. *The Horror Continues: Children Targeted.* I open my book. I try to throw myself into my reading. I know this book down to the smallest details: I must have read it twenty times. I can open it to any page and get right back into the story. It's become a clock running by itself. A circle. I said I was trying to dive back into my reading, but I have to fight my tiredness: the movement of my eyes is uncertain. The lines on the page shake. And then thoughts latch onto me like parasites. Last night's nightmare, the one that woke me at exactly 4:00 AM, plays again and again in my memory. *It's carnage. They have targeted innocence itself. Special forces are on site. The murderer seems to have been eliminated.* I see the room full of fake showers with a treadmill in the middle and then I hear the screams. Running shoes hang on the walls. The smell of gas. Trapped. Naked bodies piled up in the corners, covered by running shoes. And suddenly the doors open—freedom. An immense beach, its shore strewn with black books and bodies, abandoned, covered in algae and sea foam. The sky is a madder root red. No wind. No birds. The heat of the crematorium ovens at my back. Haze encircled mountains on the horizon. Words I don't understand come out of my mouth, a horrible sound rises and I put my hands over my ears and begin to run, but my legs won't carry me forward, they just sink into the sand, I struggle, get myself covered in dirt, fall to my knees in the sand, drained and exhausted by the impossible run. Now—silence. I look at the ocean. For some reason, I don't know why, I'm determined to count the bodies on the shore but the numbers get all mixed up and every time my count ends up back at zero.

I'm about to lift my eyes to the TV again but a man interrupts my movement. "Pick a number for me, mademoiselle, pick a number!" He's wearing a tracksuit with three white stripes. His right hand clutches a ballpoint pen. It is poised to mark up a lottery ticket. Instinctively, I answer: "Seven." *The terrorist filmed his crime. The video is already circulating on the internet.* My eyes light up. I have to see this video. "I already crossed off seven. Another? Please, mademoiselle," he continues. His smile is yellow, disquieting. "I don't know—nine," I say, irritated by the familiarity of his insistence. I have trouble talking to strangers, even more so when they get too friendly with me.

You are weak

The memories pull me under again. Shoes marked with a check are spread across the sand. I am continually buried by the abyssal sky: I slide forward then return to my starting point, so that I'm always still on the beach and escaping from it at the same time. I don't know why I picked the number seven. It doesn't matter anyway; I don't really believe in luck. The night of November 13th, we could say rather stupidly that 543 people were unlucky (I'm counting the wounded), and we could even say one among them experienced a mysterious perversion of chance: "His lifeless body lay on the ground, hit by a single bullet in the back. The bullet, in all likelihood fired by the assailants, ricocheted off the balcony before striking him through the open window of his apartment"—I read about it in *Le Parisien* a few days after the attacks. Don't be mad, but I couldn't contain my laughter, a terrible kind of laughter. Afterward, I couldn't fall asleep. I rehashed the unfolding of the event: an individual murdered at home, in an apartment of a building behind the concert hall, by a bullet shot from a window in that very hall, that happened to ricochet off the balcony, and then enter through the apartment window to finally lodge itself in the victim positioned exactly in the bullet's trajectory. "The worst of all bad luck," declared his childhood friend in the article. *What is the probability that such a drama could take place?*—the question obsessed me for the next few hours. Is it even statistically valid? When situations reveal the possibility of such absurdity, the comfortable world of numbers implodes, I told myself. So I went over all of the things that had to happen to produce exactly that kind of tragedy. We had ventured way out beyond simple bad luck, beyond *the wrong place at the wrong time*—we were right in the heart of impossibility: the worst of all bad luck. Faced with such a particular death, not to say unique in this world, I found myself trapped between two kinds of hopelessness: I had been let down as much by the power of statistics as by the power of superstition—the sheer absurdity of percentages versus the sheer cruelty of fate.

According to our information, the authorities are doing everything in their power to remove the video from social media. Users are being asked not to circulate it. This means it can be easily found, which, just for a moment and without interrogating the cause behind it, brings me joy. I type "terrorist school children throats cut" into the "video" section of the biggest search engine. I click the first link. "This video is no longer available." I keep searching. I click on the second link, the third link, the fourth link. "This video is no longer available." The fifth link finally does it. The video is one minute and fifty-two seconds long. We see a young man wearing a T-shirt with a white check on the front. He seems to be younger than twenty, with closely shaved light-brown hair, a thin nose and a generous mouth. His beauty surprises me. His French is clear and unhurried; he seems calm. The video was probably filmed on a phone: the image never stops moving; he's holding it in his right hand. He begins to brandish a knife. Then he starts filming what's happening behind him. We see children appear. I fear the worst. I cut the sound. I take another sip of beer. The young man seems possessed.

Evil precedes us

The young man raises the knife. My jaw clenches. The images that follow are unbearable, but I hold steady, before realizing that my neighbor is also watching my screen. His eyes are vacant, staring into the void. He's frightened. He saw everything (too bad for him). He leaves his seat abruptly. I'm afraid he'll go to the manager and tell him what I'm doing, that he'll make a scene. But I'm wrong: he just orders another *pastis* and buys some scratch lottery tickets. *The massacre of children is unfortunately in keeping with their logic. These people want to show us just how far they can go. To attack children is to reach the point of no return.* My gaze starts to swivel back and forth between the TV and my phone. On both screens, a massacre unfolds. But the young man's violence eventually becomes too draining for me: too much blood. I stop the video and click on the next one out of curiosity: we see two men locked in a cage in the middle of the desert. They are kneeling, hands tied behind their backs, dressed in orange jumpsuits. A hooded man, dressed entirely in black, armed with a jerry can of gasoline, approaches the cage. He sprays both prisoners with gas, they don't react. The man speaks in Arabic, his speech is subtitled in English. He proffers a few threats against Westerners before lighting a torch. The camera now remains focused on the two prisoners, we see their faces. Their eyes are closed. The man in black throws his torch with fury. Fire pours down into the cage, which instantly goes up in a blaze. Two mouths seem to scream through the flames. The bodies melt.

The testimony of the Sonderkommando returns to me. "The hair catches fire first. The skin swells with blisters that burst after a couple of seconds. The arms and legs contort. Veins and nerves tense and cause the limbs to twitch; the body is already completely ablaze. The skin has cracked open, liquid fat is running and you hear the crackle of the raging fire. You no longer see a body, just the furnace of infernal flame consuming something deep inside. The stomach bursts. The intestines and entrails fall out, and within a few minutes not a trace remains. The head takes longer to burn. Two little blue flames blaze in the eye sockets. The eyes are consumed along with the base of the brain, while the tongue is carbonized in the mouth. The whole process lasts about twenty minutes, and then a body—a world—is reduced to ashes. You have to harden your heart, suffocate all sensitivity, blunt and dull any painful feeling. You have to renounce the atrocious suffering that tears through your limbs like a hurricane. You have

to transform yourself into an automaton. Not see anything. Not feel anything." I put my cell phone down on
the counter, stunned by the savagery I'd just witnessed.
I told you not long ago that we need to fight for beauty,
but here I am throwing myself once again to its opposite. I gave in to violence when I could have avoided it: I
succumbed to crime when I could have not. I'm without
a doubt no better than these criminals, no, I'm no better
than these terrorists.

Could you have really

As I sip my beer, I follow the development of the
operations underway. The news channel is doing all it
can to offer viewers the best vantage points: the camera stubbornly films the entrance to the public school,
slowly panning from left to right and then from high
to low. The shots are carefully composed and give a
nice perspective on the crime scene. All around the
front entrance, protected by a security cordon as well
as a large green tent that hides a portion of the sidewalk, law enforcement officials come and go, dressed
in bulletproof vests, armed and hooded, cutting across
the screen. Extremely nervous policemen motion to the
journalists to keep their distance; there's anger in the
way they move their arms. *The death toll is rising. It now
appears that three children are counted among the dead,
not just two.* My book is still resting on the counter. I
try again at last to dive back into my reading, I try to

fall into its world. I read: "The road, which was terrible and full of pot-holes, went steeply downhill here," but the screens that surround me annihilate every attempt I make to focus. I close the book again and fix my gaze on the big screen in front of me. I imagine the whole country glued to their TVs and social media—millions of retinas going dry, unable to blink as they watch the swift succession of images. My phone vibrates. A notification informs me that the social media site to which I've been loyal for a few years has just added an "anti-suicide" alert: you can now, with a single click, bring the dark thoughts or alarming states of your virtual friends to the attention of teams standing by 24/7. It reminds me of a report I saw last week on an anti-suicide brigade in South Korea charged with saving people trying to jump from the Mapo bridge in Seoul, *one of the most popular suicide spots in the city*, as the report puts it. Doesn't matter—that type of information isn't particularly useful right now (in the not too distant future, though, it's entirely imaginable).

I think of my sister, Etty. I wonder where she could be at this moment and what she might be doing. Is she smiling? Crying? Cursing me for my absence? Does she miss me, is she angry with me—oh well, what's done is done. Etty is probably lucky to be blind. It spares her the same inconceivable violence I can't seem to resist. She's two years younger than me and she's never seen the world the way that I see it with my own eyes. Or, rather, it's me who's never seen and heard the world the way that she sees and hears it with her whole body. It's funny—my sister needs a cane to walk down the street, she can't read a book without touching it, I have to tell her whether clothes look good on her or not, I have to cook all her hot meals out of fear that she'll burn herself, but she's so much wiser than I am.

If someday my sister gets into a situation, if she finds herself in the middle of a terrorist attack, who will be able to help her? No one. One of these days, one of the two of us will probably be confronted with a situation of extreme violence. If it's her, someone is going to need to save her. In any event, even if Etty wasn't blind, I'd still have done all I could to make sure she didn't stumble on these horrors—videos and photos of massacres. Not that it would have made much of a difference. She would be sucked in, too. And let's be honest: I would have been the first one to show her, I'd want to share my feeling of horror. I wouldn't just want her to see, to see what is being inflicted on her generation, for her to be shocked like I am, but I'd especially want it to be me, her sister, that shows her the degradation, the decline—me and no one else. My sister wasn't born blind: at the age of six, meningitis took her sight. She could have lost use of her legs, her neck, her speech—in the end it turned out to be the use of her eyes. For a long time I tried to figure out the last thing she ever saw: what was her last vision. Still today I sometimes ask her the question. *What was the last thing you saw*, I ask. But she tells me she doesn't remember. And that question bothers her.

My cell phone vibrates again on the counter, the screen lights up. *Syria. An underground library: a shelter from the bombings.* The presence of the words *library* and *bombings* in the same sentence attracts my attention. I can't resist the urge to click on the article. "The library is located several meters underground, in the city of Darayya, near Damascus. And while the bombings rage outside, the establishment remains open. In August 2012, the city became the setting of the most significant massacre carried out in Syria. More than 330 bodies were discovered. The inhabitants are reputed to be hostile to the regime. And it's underground that they take refuge to read and to hide from the explosions. A last bastion protecting the cultural heritage of the population, you can find fearsome books like Cervantes's *Don Quixote* or Márquez's *One Hundred Years of Solitude,* all translated into Arabic: in total, about eleven thousand books gathered from personal collections and bookstores." Three days ago, before getting on the metro, I passed the bookstore where I've been buying my books since I was fourteen. It was closed: a FOR SALE sign was glued to the window. My heart contracted. Impossible, I said to myself. Not this one. Not this bookstore.

How far: to the point of suffocation

Who knows what we'll end up with in place of this lost paradise—yes it was a paradise, a kind of paradise, for Etty and I, it was a little oasis of peace in the heart of the city. Maybe it'll be an optometrist, a grocery store, a fast-food place, a bank, an insurance company—no, I'm leaning toward optometrist, they've been popping up everywhere in the capital over the last few months, I see them everywhere. It'd be doubly painful for my sister since she's blind, blind and frighteningly lucid (I told you, she sees everything, that sister of mine. She sees everything and says nothing). I shouldn't be morose. I shouldn't lean into an obnoxious nostalgia, not at my age, it would be stupid (the world is big, the possibilities almost endless), *one Parisian death is worth ten thousand others*, but for a bookstore closed, how many victims, for a book unread, how many deaths, for a memory lost, how many deaths. Books are black holes, capable of lifting you out of this life, they are just as much the many lives that wait to intrude on you, to change you, to devastate you. Because what even is a book without light or fury—I don't know of any. Books have the obligation to strike you like lightning, I'd even say this devastation is exactly what I ask of them: open me, carry me, wake me up. I ask them to wage a war on this whole world, to embrace and destroy suffering, and to transfigure my thinking . . . I believe this is what I've always demanded of a book. How many times have I said to my sister, how many times have I said *this book is killing me, it killed me, you have to read it!* Truthfully—not that often, maybe twenty times, not many more, I said it about *Under the Volcano*, I said it about *The Sound and the Fury*, about *Absalom, Absalom!*, I said it about *Madame Bovary*, about *The Legend of Saint Julian the Hospitaller*, Saint Julian killed me, I told her, and I said the same thing—read, reread, and read again—about *The Castle*, about *The Metamorphosis*, about *Moby Dick* and "Bartleby, the Scrivener," about *Lolita* and *Catcher in the Rye*. I said it about *Beyond Good and Evil*, about *Fatelessness*, I said it about the Gospels, and about *On the Way to Language*, and the Bible, *The Pale King*, and about *The Unpardonable*, about *The Nerve Meter*, about *Illuminations*, and *Ulysses*, and so many others . . . Life is as interminable as it is scandalously short, and one must chase its treasures. I've said: "Etty, I have to read this aloud to you because it killed me" and kills me still, and what kills me is the horizon these books give shape to, they lead us and follow behind, always both out in front and walking alongside: they receive, they deepen, they extend what I am and what I've been, all these books— all these worlds.

I lose my way. In my state of exhaustion, this is inevitable (if my calculations are correct, I slept three

hours and thirty minutes last night). The weather fore-
cast comes on the TV. The weather lady is a brunette
with curly hair and a leather skirt. I hear her say: *The
weekend will be unsettled. We can see rain coming through
with various low-pressure systems circulating over France.
Rain once again, then, in low lying areas with a less exposed
coastline—the Aquitaine coast—as well as in the lower valley of the Rhone right down to the Mediterranean, more
intense storms over Corsica, and beware of freezing fog in
the North, the cool air is coming from that direction and it
could make for slippery road conditions.* I gave up on sun
a long time ago—here sunshine is just an accident that
sometimes happens to you.

I'm starting to get hungry. It's 6:40 PM, I wonder what
I'll end up eating tonight. In my head, I go through
the contents of my refrigerator. Next to the half empty
bottles of soda, now deprived of their bubbles, there's
ketchup, organic apples wrapped in cellophane, and old
pickles floating in vinegar. *There will also be snow in the
mountains and at lower altitudes as the cold air progres-
sively spreads. The disturbances will subside as they reach the
Pyrenees, snow also at six hundred meters in the Auvergne
high country, at four hundred meters over the Jura, at six
hundred meters in its Alpine zone, at one thousand five
hundred meters over Corsica.* Snow. I love the snow. As
a child, I used to eat it. I see the compartments of my

fridge, their form is carved into me. They smell of dirty snow—the blackened snow of parking lots, of the bottom of a ski hill. A woman sits down at the counter on my right. She wears a midnight blue headscarf, her eyes are bright and intimately focused on the phone she holds horizontal in her hands. I can read the sentences as she scrolls through them, down and then up, with her ring finger. My phone vibrates. I just got an email. It's a message from the CEO of Eurostar: groups of refugees have been dying regularly in the Eurotunnel, causing unfortunate delays. It's a difficult infestation to eradicate. But the measures being taken all seem very convincing: "Increased SNCF agent and police presence along the high-speed line used by our trains [. . .] A rapid reaction procedure is in place in the event of any intrusion on the tracks [. . .] Clearing of the vegetation in the areas surrounding the routes to prevent any possible intruders from hiding (already underway) and the ongoing installation of additional fencing by Eurotunnel to ensure the security of the high-speed line in the areas in question." The message ends on a convivial note: "Together, these measures will enable a significant reduction in the risks of service disturbances and will permit rapid reactions in the event of the repetition of this kind of incident. Rest assured that we and our partners are doing all we can to guarantee reliable service in order to meet your expectations." I place the message in the trash like I do for all advertisements: it's been a habit of mine for several years now. A feeling of discouragement latches on to me. Maybe also a bit of anger. I have trouble naming the emotion exactly. It's distant. I put my phone back down on the counter. I return to my reading, page thirty-eight, *Insane thoughts obsess me until dusk I thought I was bleeding I thought he had struck me with his ax,* the unbound violence of the speaker melting and flowing right to my heart *you don't have to if you don't want to.* The television, the phone, the book—my brain is torn between these three worlds. *The grasslands undulated up until the first slopes of the volcanoes before disappearing behind a screen of black night. What's certain is that we can imagine the carnage. Children. It's unnamable.*

*

November 13th was the largest massacre in France since Oradour-sur-Glane. I raise my eyes. Gilles Kepel is on the set. Oradour. I remember. At Oradour, at the Bataclan, the few survivors hid under the bodies of the dead waiting for the threat to be neutralized, which essentially means that the dead saved their lives. "I personally cleared out the church," declared Sergeant Boos on June 11th, 1944, after the murderous fire meticulously planned by the German army. Cleared out, not cleaned up: unlike the Bataclan, there was no flesh or blood, only dust, with the exception of the few bodies that remained intact—"In the sacristy, two little boys of twelve or thirteen held each other in a tight embrace, united in a last shudder of horror. In the confessional, an even smaller boy was seated, his head bent forward." I didn't find these words skimming through a yellowed history book: all you need to do is type Oradour-sur-Glane into Google. Wikipedia has all the necessary information. "The remains of a child of eight or ten months rested in a baby carriage [...] Here and there were bits of skulls, legs, arms, ribs, a foot still in a shoe," testified a survivor. I learned these sentences by heart a few years ago: not out of a sense of good conscience or curiosity, but to study for a ninth grade history quiz on the horrors of the Occupation: I wanted to get at least a fifteen out of twenty, a sixteen if possible, to save my average. I knew that in evoking such morbid and historically accurate details on my test, I was shifting the odds in my favor. "On the 11th and 12th of June, groups of SS returned to Oradour to bury the bodies and render their identification impossible." Next to the picture of the pit at the Bataclan on my bedroom wall, maybe I should have added a photo of the ruins of the church at Oradour-sur-Glane. But you know how this goes: if I put up the massacre of Oradour, then I have to add the massacre of Tulle (117 dead, out of which ninety were hung); and if I add Tulle, then I have to add the massacre of Calviac, and it'll never end—my wall, like my memory, is not big enough to contain all the catastrophes. So we must always show humility and rely on a good sense of organization: most atrocities will slip between my fingers. It's my job to not hold them back.

My phone vibrates. Another email, but this time it's from my best friend. It's been two months since I heard from her—not a word.

Ava, I spent a week with Paul in an apartment building near the Gobelins. A week of loving piously and playfully, like children. Our relationship has an incestuousness to it; we look like brother and sister, there is a mirrored sensitivity and sensuality between us. Finding ourselves together again is so bittersweet. I am sad to be home. I write to you under the heavy, gray skies of Brussels—a reflection of the fury I carry inside. I want it to break open, I dream of a thunderstorm, of a torrent of words. Love has made me fragile, disarmed me completely. Paul lulls me into a delicious forgetfulness of the outside world, and I wait for only one thing: to allow myself to be swallowed up by his words and his body. My solitude weighs on me because it's an unfinished state of being. I feel myself ablaze only in fusion with another. That's how it is with my friendships and my loves—even with our correspondence. Everything brings me back to this painful intuition—I am nothing if not a vector, a dark and negative energy. I'm permanently nauseous. I don't know where it comes from. I want to vomit words, to vomit love, to purge myself of something immense. I drink a great deal but the alcohol disgusts me. I want to feel light, to be bathed in light. I'm afraid of withering. If you only knew . . . I spent the evening looking at master's programs at Sciences-Po, telling myself I should go back to school, to a prestigious program, if possible, so I don't have to feel ashamed. My sister gave me a lecture today—she told me I was crazy to stay in Brussels, she said what the hell are you waiting for, *that to stay here was a death wish and that we were "destined for greatness." Oh, I'd so love to believe her. What to do with my body, with my spirit—with this mind that can think? And about that—why do people choose to do a master's in Public Administration? I want someone to explain it to me, I want to be told I'm wrong to live in the moment, stubbornly preferring freedom, and that what young people should really be doing, instead of gratuitous and unjustified wandering, is getting a master's in Public Administration and International Relations. It's not too late for me, Ava, I can catch up to the group, I can fall back in line with them, but I'm afraid, afraid of remaining on the outside my whole life. I feel like I was sacrificed before I even had the chance to realize; I feel like I am destined to live by false, forged breaths. I am not a philosopher or an artist (in spite of my dreams); I am nothing but a poor beating heart! It wouldn't matter if I moved away, went on long travels, or won the respect of my peers—nothing will stop my fall. I take no pleasure in writing these sentences, and maybe I'm wrong to send them to you. To me they seem heavy, made in the image of my sorrow. What is it that gnaws away at us like this? Pride? What is that feeble word we use—depression? I've always hated it! It is empty. It's a cliché. A pure cliché. I want to find another word. I want to invent a language to tell you my pain, and I want you to tell me that we'll be enough, that we'll be okay. I wonder if I still believe in signs. I'd like to believe that, for the time it takes to write a letter, I have some peace. Help me. Tell me what I should do. I feel powerless. Lost. I no longer know if I'm sane or crazy, stupid or smart, beautiful or a disgrace. Sometimes I no longer know if I'm even telling the truth. The joy, ever deferred, of not knowing how to get through the next moment.*

x

Adèle

A lump rises in my throat. She is saying *help me*. She wants me to show her the way. But how can you help a being who thinks and breathes exactly like you? A profound empathy for every word uttered, whose birth and the incompleteness I can see, given over to the emptiness of an insurmountable present. I have nothing to respond but *I understand.* No other answer, and this makes my feelings of sadness and love for her grow. I'm limited to such a meager solidarity. I must nonetheless tell the story of how I met Adèle. It was twelve years ago. I remember the courtyard of our middle school, her cold, hawk-like gaze, solitary, lost in an indecipherable language, dressed in silence. Adèle sat down next to me. We were waiting for the tide of humans in front of the cafeteria entrance to recede. You always had to wait in line for a half an hour just to get a revolting meal of defrosted french fries, defrosted sausages, and defrosted bread. Often, we gave up altogether: we would stay seated on the stone slabs of the courtyard, far from the crowd. I remember her gentleness and her maturity, and also the wound that lived in her, murmuring to mine that our paths, from then on, would be linked. She told me about her many moves, of her feeling of not having a home, and of being thrown into the world, with no sense of belonging—something that resonated with me in an unsettling yet redeeming way, because, for the first time, I had encountered a soul born of the same exile.

3

I'm sorry. I'm not pretty enough.
KATELYN NICOLE DAVIS, age twelve

The young woman is still there. Her elbows rest on the
counter. Her eyes are fixed on her phone screen. She's
playing a video game. I know the game by heart. I've
played it myself an incalculable number of times. The
hero's name is Trevor. He's always dressed the same, in
a leather jacket and a pair of worn jeans. On the TV, a
new guest has arrived and is settling in. It's been two
years since I last played *GTA*. In this moment, I realize
how much I missed Trevor. *Madame Politi, hello, you're
a journalist, what can you tell us about the phenomenon
of radicalization that's affecting our youth?* Trevor grips
his pump-action shotgun tightly. He runs right into the
middle of the street, blocking traffic before stealing a

car. *There has been a dizzying loss of stable reference points, young people are looking for meaning. As I've recently written, never has the number of French citizens implicated in Jihadist networks been so significant, and the trend seems far from changing course.* It all comes back to me. Trevor was making his way through the immensity of the city. The faster the car went, the more I felt I was going too slow. Trevor ran red lights, he scraped against trucks and souped-up race cars, crushing everything in his path: strollers, children, old people, women, drug lords, wild animals, and pets, no matter the species, age, gender, and appearance—the world was a game. *These young people are angry, they feel abandoned.* A few minutes into the game, the experience of absorption was so intense I became Trevor. I was no longer flesh and blood. At dawn, there was only silence. The sun burned in the sky. I stole dozens of cars; I killed hundreds of people. It was all easy, fun—free. *The Western world has raised them in a very serious climate of economic violence. Leaving to fight a war may give them an unprecedented sense of having real freedom, they finally feel useful, connected to an absolute cause, defenders of a voice that breaks with everything that's been imposed on them. In reality, it's not a holy war, it's an economic and moral one.* I wandered through the roads above the city. I went off-roading, and took mountain paths, penetrating into the flora and the fauna: I sacrificed fawns, rabbits, deer. As soon as I got tired of driving, I'd total the car against a tree or get out of the vehicle and empty all my bullets into the motor. The car would catch fire and then explode. *These terrorists only want one thing: to spill blood on our soil.* Sometimes I'd let myself die. In a fight or an explosion. It never mattered because I always came back to life. The light across the whole screen would fade to darkness, then a blood-red sentence would appear, it said: YOU'RE DEAD, and then right below: PLAY AGAIN. I'd click and wait twelve seconds for the game to start over. *We haven't seen anything close to what they're capable of yet.* And voilà, Trevor would pop up all over again. I'd get back on the road. I stopped cars on the boulevard, I threw their drivers out. There were two categories of victims: those who fled and those who fought back. I executed the cowards with a bullet to the back. But I fought the ones who resisted with my bare hands. That didn't make much of a difference for them—I was always stronger. I destroyed their noses, their teeth, their abdomens. Once my victims were lifeless on the ground, I'd trash their body with the help of a bat or a hammer. A pool of blood would spread across the asphalt: if it was nighttime, the flow shimmered with reflections of the moon (the programmers took the aesthetic details seriously, something I couldn't help but admire). After the violence, I felt a strange sense of relief. *Never, in the history of our country, have we faced such a threat. One from our compatriots, our fellow citizens, going abroad to indoctrinate themselves in terror and horror in order to eventually strike their own country.* I got back on the road. I was free as I traveled, free in my solitude, and free in my crimes. One second was equal to a minute and one minute was equal to an hour. I passed from day to night in twenty-four minutes. *Terrorism is international, young people all over the world are leaving their families to go enlist in these organizations.* Sometimes I'd see a beach on the horizon. I'd go swim in the ocean. Sometimes I'd commit suicide. No big deal: I knew that resurrection was right around the corner. No more fear: there's nothing but the endless city and my own omnipotence. Finally, people respected me. I raise my eyes to the TV. The journalist's speech is accompanied by extremely precise graphs, bar charts, parabolas, pie charts—a science unto itself: the science of terror.

The boss has just realized that my glass is empty; I'm determined, however, to have just one drink. "Allez, here, I'll make you a cocktail of the day, a bloody mary," he says, with the eyes of a tempter: "It's on the house." "Avec plaisir," I answer, knowing full well it's a mistake: a cocktail is even worse than a second beer. What's more, I don't like vodka, but often I don't know how to say no. *Monsieur Thomson, thank you for joining us. You're also a journalist. The question I have for you is this: what are these young French people hoping for when they leave to become*

Jihadists?—"It is Islam that restores our dignity because France has humiliated us": *This sentiment summarizes the question of identity well enough. They think something prophetic will take place in Syria, which is to say, the coming of the messiah, and that those who align themselves with the right side will go to paradise, while the others will be doomed to hell, so there's a feeling of urgency; they are seeing history through apocalyptic, eschatological eyes.* While he's speaking, the two screens behind him play an advertisement for a car company. A gray diamond against a yellow background appears, under which is written: "TAKE CHARGE OF YOUR OWN JOURNEY." The slogan appears, disappears, reappears. The server places the cocktail on the counter. I thank him. I taste the cocktail. I hide my disappointment. *Social media has changed the image of Jihad by making it more accessible. By putting their lives on display, Jihadists make Jihad more appealing and more accessible than the Afghani caves of the past. Online, people joke about a decapitation video with an Al-Qaeda fighter; they discuss the best pair of "Air Maxes" for going to war in.* I used to wear Air Maxes. They were black and red. Uniquely comfortable. I change my focus to my phone, contemplating the darkened screen. One night, I wasn't able to sleep (I was ruminating on my endlessness doubts), so to distract myself I started to research the technical specifications of my cell phone, saying to myself: isn't it true that it's strange to spend so much time with an object without knowing what it's made of? I'll tell you: it's made of praseodymium, gadolinium, terbium, indium oxide, tin dioxide, and potassium salts; the battery is made of lithium; and the microphone is made of nickel, tin and lead. The microchip is made of silicon, arsenic, and phosphorus. The body is made of magnesium. One hundred and fifty-eight millimeters in length, seventy-eight millimeters wide, and seven millimeters thick. Sometimes I still contemplate my phone as though I was discovering it for the first time—I turn it over in my hands and gaze at the half-eaten apple: they say it's an homage to the one, filled with cyanide, that killed Alan Turing. Sometimes I imagine that cyanide is hidden inside that tiny half-eaten apple, that it has infiltrated the object and is penetrating the skin on my fingers and palms, spreading all the way into my veins. I remember an article in "Santé," the health section of *Le Figaro*, an article with radical content. I learned these sentences off by heart: "By analyzing the molecules present on the surface of a cell phone, it is possible to create a profile of the lifestyle of the device's owner. With every use, the user deposits molecules from their outer layer of skin on the surface of the phone. By analyzing these molecules it is thus possible to generate a composite portrait of the lifestyles of cell phone users. The molecules found have made it possible to determine if the owner is male or female, to determine their preference for beer or wine, or even to know if they take any medications. And there's no point in wiping down your device to clear away all traces of your lifestyle: certain molecules remain present on the device for several months." It's not worth fearing the robots: transhumanism has already been with us for a long time. It's here on this counter; in this little object covered with tiny bits of skin containing my deoxyribonucleic acid; it's in the couple of centimeters linking my gaze to the screens above me; it's in the friction produced by the movement of the electronic microchip in my watch against the skin of my left wrist; it's in my memories, number after number, in the death statistics I've learned by heart thanks to Wikipedia. It's everywhere—I'm telling you.

*

New notification. It never ends. *A girl of twelve live streams her own suicide.* I click on the article. *Katelyn Nicole Davis, a young girl of twelve, took her own life, live in front of her virtual friends. The suicide, witnessed millions of times, has provoked the indignation of the American authorities, powerless against the widespread circulation of the video.* No need to read on. Following my time-honored ritual, I go to the search engine and type in the key words: *video suicide katelyn*. I find the video within a few seconds. I turn on the sound at low volume. Katelyn Nicole Davis is speaking to her online friends. She's alone in her room. Her first words are: *fuck I don't know*. What Katelyn Nicole Davis says, during those interminable minutes, is that she'd prefer not to live in this world. The teenager cries, disclosing she'd been sexually abused and was having trouble at school, before concluding: *I'm sorry, I'm not pretty enough*. The young girl goes outside and sets up the camera in front of a tree; we see her climbing the tree; she ties a rope to it. A stool is already there, in front of the tree: everything has been carefully prepared. The young girl climbs onto the stool and adjusts the rope around her neck. She says her goodbyes to her family and friends, moaning and whimpering, nose full of snot; then she falls into nothingness. For twenty minutes, her shoes hang in front of the camera: the body is stiff. Her friends rush to share the video: horror is vanquished by fascination. In a few short hours, Katelyn Nicole Davis' suicide has been around the world several times over. It's not so much the death of a twelve-year-old girl that provokes the frenzy: it's the powerlessness of the authorities to delete what the public never should have seen. It's not Katelyn that has taken her own life, it's our screens that exterminated her. It's the Instagram filters that hide pimples; it's the Kim Kardashian makeup tutorials; it's diet culture. Yes, let's talk about thinness—modernity's extraordinary asceticism. Because being beautiful is being thin. And being thin is about getting down to the essentials. I am obsessed with thinness: at least as much as with sports. To be thin is to be pure—or at least to strive for a form of purity.

It would be a lie to say I don't understand this young girl. I do understand her: I understand the suicide of Katelyn Nicole Davis. I'd even say: I sympathize with her. I often find myself ugly. I'd even say that the more I feel the need to be beautiful, the more ugly I feel. Which means that more and more I find myself feeling ugly, because more and more we have to show we're beautiful. I'm twenty-five years old, which means that I have an obligation to be beautiful, or at least to be palatable (some say: *alright, or good enough*). If I'm not cute at my age, or at least fine, what does that mean for when I turn thirty-five; what does that mean for when I turn forty-five; what does that mean for when the ordeal of the half-century comes, the big five-oh (when we pole-vault into the final half of our lives)? We spend our time trying to be beautiful—or trying to stay beautiful—for the simple reason that things'll never be better than they are right now: I won't get prettier with time; with a lot of luck, I might stay almost as good—but all things considered, it's downhill from here. Katelyn Nicole Davis went straight for the essential: she short-circuited beauty. She said to us: I don't have to become beautiful or be good because, first of all, I find myself irremediably ugly, and second: soon I'll be good for eternity. Katelyn didn't take her own life: it's our world that exterminated her.

I contemplate my cocktail. I won't be touching it again. My eyes return to rest on the TV. I can't help but admire the professionalism of this channel: they push the repetition of their segments as far as humanly possible. It's almost 7:00 PM. Tiredness overtakes me. I pay for my drink, thank the server again, apologizing for not being able to finish the poison. Before leaving, I go to the bathroom. I run water over my face. I look in the mirror. I don't recognize myself. There are days full of uncertainty, threatening days, when the few things that should be sure and taken for granted are nowhere to be found. Today is one of those days when the foundations are shaken. When we find ourselves naked, overcome with vertigo. There is no peace. There is no *other shore* across the river. There is only one world, and no curtain behind which to seek refuge.

Everything that we have ever loved
will always be all around us.
GÉRARD DE NERVAL

The meaning of the world is outside
of the world, which is to say that the
outside of the world is on the inside.
LUDWIG WITTGENSTEIN

We learn to experience and to endure
loss and that is, in my view, a science.
ROBERT WALSER

III

1

My phone only has five percent battery left: absolute solitude is imminent. I'm hungry. My head is spinning. I walk toward Gare de l'Est. I go into a fast food place. A smell of cold grease and bleach radiates. The floor is covered with white tiling. It's damp. My shoes squeak as I walk. I scan the faces around me. You never know who might blow themselves up. You never know who might pull out a weapon. I go up to an automatic kiosk with a touch screen. I scroll through pictures of hamburgers. I have no desire to eat meat. I haven't been eating meat for a couple months now—the idea of swallowing a dead being is repugnant to me. Maybe only because of the blood. Blood blood blood. Why this obsession. I select a medium fries and a bottle of water. I pay with my credit card. The kiosk spits out a ticket bearing the number 3758.

I move up to the counter and hand my ticket to an employee. While I wait, I turn my head toward the back of the room. Two screens hang on the wall. They are playing the same news station as the TV at the bar-tabac. I pick up my order of fries and a bottle of mineral water in a little recyclable brown paper bag without handles. I go to sit down on a bench of beige Formica, near the washrooms, in front of one of the TVs. I eat the fries one by one; they're hard, probably just defrosted this morning and cooked a second time a half an hour ago. I struggle to discern their flavor. To compensate for their blandness, I dip a couple in a puddle of ketchup. Then I think of my sister. I still can't believe I refused to get on the plane. I still can't believe that I refused to go with her to the funeral. I've probably disappointed my whole family. So what? I always aggravate my own suffering; I aggravate all difficult things. After all, my sister and I have always been really lucky—until now. Like millions of others: we are survivors. I remember my sister's eyes when I told her I wasn't coming to the funeral. Her look—wounded, cloudy, pupilless—pierced me through with sadness and shame. I let her go to the airport. I let her go alone, why? Because otherwise, I would have cried, I would have dissolved into tears in front of my sister—pitiful. It's always hard for me to give in to such a display of feelings. So I cried as soon as she closed the door to the apartment, a pathetic torrent of tears I could not restrain. *Stay tuned—we'll be back after a short break.* I lift my head toward the TV.

The channel's logo fills the screen. Three white letters on a blue background. Unsettling orchestral music with a driving rhythm blares. A succession of images follows: a tank gives way to the face of the American President which gives way to the face of a soccer player which gives way to a protest which gives way to a high-speed car chase which gives way to the red carpet at Cannes which gives way to air strikes which give way to the face of the French President which gives way to a helicopter on fire which gives way to the face of Leonardo DiCaprio. After this interlude, the ads begin. The first one extols the merits of a particular pregnancy test. Two women sit at a table together. One confides to the other that she is pregnant, while brandishing the test. They exchange a smile. I think of the children dead this afternoon, and of the parents who have lost their progeny. I grimace, repulsed, then laugh nervously. Again, my cell phone vibrates, I take it out of my pocket, a notification flashes on the screen—*Terrorist group succeeds in acquiring means for the production of an atomic bomb.* A man in ratty clothing comes out of the washroom. He is carrying plastic bags and holding his cell phone in his right hand: a model identical to my own. We all pretty much want the same thing. Whether East or West; North or South. I understand the necessity of acquiring the atomic bomb—at least as well as I understand the need to get a cell phone. It is a right, the right to be respected and feared. What's more, my cell phone has chemical elements similar to those found in the components of a bomb—in lesser quantities, sure, but for that reason alone I respect it: I know that it is dangerous.

To each his bomb to each his border

The man sits down on the bench under the screens. He looks deeply drunk. I think of Geoffrey Firmin, the hero of my bedside book. This man resembles him. So much so that I could be dreaming. I've spent so much time with Geoffrey Firmin that I just don't know anymore. To enter that far into the experience of reading is to put an end to the fiction of it. I've shouldered the burden of Geoffrey Firmin since I was eighteen. I have carried him, toiled with that burden—from the majesty of his memories to his final coming apart, been witness to his alcoholic and sentimental drift, in the end a kind of esoteric one, since Geoffrey Firmin was not saved—or maybe I'm wrong, maybe he was saved at the last moment by a revelation, before succumbing to the definitive call of the abyss: carried off by the void behind a scrawny dog's carcass. Geoffrey Firmin taught me a thing or two. And the worst of what he showed me was probably the closeness of our natures.

You aren't like Geoffrey, you aren't like Geoffrey

To dominate your fears; to dominate your life, dominate a being, dominate a people; to commit to love, commit to light, commit to a team, commit to a value;

to annihilate solitude, annihilate cruelty, annihilate divisions, annihilate a being, annihilate a religion, annihilate a people. I finish my fries. I suck my grease and salt covered fingers. The voice of my sister returns to haunt me. She insults me. All because she must be sending me negative energy from across the ocean. I imagine her there, in Neuquén, just arrived at our grandmother's house, worn out by the trip, trying somehow to console my mother. She inhales the scent of the flowers in the garden. She breathes in the sky. Alone. She misses me as I miss her.

It's time that you left

My hunger hasn't gone away. I'm now thinking of getting an ice cream. Vanilla or strawberry. Atomic bomb. Inside my head, these two words are excoriating one another. I cannot come to understand them. More precisely, I cannot come to understand that humanity could have gone so far in the possibilities of destruction. Atomic bomb. I picture my plane ticket on the desk in my room. I assured my parents that I would get my money back from the airline (I haven't called them yet but it has to be done soon). It's not even really a problem since I have up to twenty-four hours after take-off to get my money back. Although this ticket has a connection: Paris to São Paulo; São Paulo to Buenos Aires. If I remember correctly, the São Paulo to Buenos Aires flight took off this morning at 8:00 AM, Paris time.

So I have until 8:00 AM tomorrow to get my refund. Exchangeable and refundable: it's written right on the ticket. Of course, I could then still take the plane tonight (as long as the flight isn't full). But why am I even thinking about this? No reason—I'm staying. I will remain. I am going to get my refund. A vanilla ice cream with Oreo pieces: it's possible. *You're a coward*, the last sentence uttered by my sister last night, before she cleared out. Poor thing. If she had known. If she had known how much that word wounded me, she would never have said it. We spend our time destroying beings. With a look. With a thought. With a gesture. With a comment. With silence. With the defeat of attentiveness; little waves, irradiant, seemingly harmless, which, thrown in the face of strangers or loved ones, end up killing them.

All the same, you won't do it; leave, you won't do it, I tell myself. *Atomic bomb*. How could we? I am beginning to suffocate, not only in this place, not only in this city. The dead, the paranoia, the threats have gotten to me. Injustice and fear have come to weigh on me. On me, who thought I could just close my eyes, but the anguish persists. A vanilla ice cream, that's what I'll get, but a small one, or else I'll get sick—I held back my tears in front of Etty, I held them back until the last second, and the moment she closed the door, alone in the apartment after I let her leave, I said to myself: my life is fucked, my life is over and I am beyond redemption and I will never do anything, I will never really do anything because I don't have what it takes—I lied and in return life has given me illusion.

Shut up

Forgive me: I'm just tired. I get up. I go up to the kiosk. I'm alone in front of the screen. I look for the desserts. *Coward, you're a coward*, I hear in my head. There are four flavors available. I don't even know if I want dessert. I don't even know if I want an ice cream. Taking control of my own destiny—I don't know if I'm even capable of that anymore. As a child, I gave it no thought. Around fifteen, I started to believe it was possible. It was this glimmer even in the heart of night. My phone vibrates. All of this because of some pretty dubious readings (*Moby Dick. The Songs of Maldoror. Illuminations.* It's not like they help you become more normal). And here we are, but little by little, I'm getting on the straight and narrow: I'm revising my plans. Is this what getting older is, compromising your destiny and then producing a sanitized report describing how it happened?

Never never never you hear me

I give up on dessert. I give up on checking my phone. I leave the fast-food place. My sister must pity me for what I'm becoming. That being said, I don't know if she was ever proud. She's still never told me: I'm proud of you. The day is fading—the sky darkens to rosy tones. Terrified to accept. Terrified to understand. Terrified to fail. Terrified to share. Terrified to think. Terrified to not think. Terrified to believe—terrified to not believe in anything. Terrified of people. Terrified of absence. Terrified to breathe, to suffocate, to sleep.

In the street, I spot eight soldiers. They seem friendly and innocent. It's possible I'm not thinking straight—I haven't got the strength to fear anyone anymore.

Don't succumb to exhaustion

I don't really know what's happening to me. Only one word persists: leave. It's becoming an obsession. I take line seven toward La Courneuve. I don't have my passport. I get out at Stalingrad. I rush to get to my apartment (I went into my sister's room. It was empty. I grabbed two books, a T-shirt, underwear, a phone charger, my toiletry bag, a sweater, and a pair of black pants. I put my things in a duffel bag. I took my passport and a wad of pesos kept preciously in an old iron box. I drank a big glass of water. I went out, I raced down six flights of stairs). I get back on line seven. I get out at Opera station. There are soldiers in front of the stairs. I don't look at their faces, but keep my gaze fixed on their guns.

I wait for the bus to Roissy. I get on the bus. I close my eyes. My heart is beating exceptionally hard. I want to forget where I am. I think of my family. They are the only beings in the world who actually matter in my life.

Blood ties are not chosen. They are exigent. From time to time, I reopen my eyes. I look at the faces that surround me. I wonder what their destinations might be. The bus driver is terrible. He accelerates and brakes suddenly, producing jolts where there should be smoothness. To distract myself from my nausea, I mentally recite poems.

I get to the airport at 7:05 PM. The terminal is peppered with patrolling soldiers. Bullet-proof vests. Assault rifles. I don't have any bags to check. I walk toward the self-service check-in kiosks. I type in my name and reservation number: 19407. Tonight's flight isn't full. Inside, I feel an explosion of happiness. I modify my reservation. At the very moment that the machine prints my new ticket, my euphoria evaporates. A vague sense of gloom washes over me. Suddenly, I have a desire to go home.

Stay go stay go stay

I find myself in the departures area. People are saying their goodbyes. There are tears and smiles. *No one is holding me back.* A giant screen, about sixty feet long and thirty feet wide, is hanging above the immigration desks. It's an ad for Dior: a young, half-naked woman sprays herself with perfume while spinning around. She smiles mischievously. I think of the piles of human bodies asphyxiated with gas in *Son of Saul* (I haven't been able to forget certain shots from the film, they haunt me like the November dead). The ad ends and restarts. I find it hard to take my eyes off the screen. There are fourteen people ahead of me. I patiently wait my turn and then I present my passport to customs. The officer looks it over indifferently (less than five seconds). I take my passport back. I pass through customs—with a thought for the hundreds of thousands of deaths engendered by this *open sesame!* of no one's dreams. I stand in line to go through security. Travelling is no longer movement—it's waiting. You have to take off your belt, your shoes, your watch, and empty your pockets of change. I'm not wearing a watch, I left it on my desk before leaving. When it's my turn, I slip off my jacket, my shoes, and I put my bag in a plastic tray; the security guards help me place the tray on a rubber conveyor belt. When the moment comes to pass through the metal detector, I feel afraid. I always expect the alarm to go off, but it doesn't. A woman takes me aside. She touches my arms, my armpits, my stomach, my thighs, my legs. She's wearing beige latex gloves. I don't feel the warmth of her palms. She tells me: "Ok." I don't answer. I feel slightly violated. I wait for my bag to pass through the X-ray machine. I put my shoes back on. I pick up my bag. I watch the strangers around me, beltless, shoeless: humiliated.

I go into Duty-Free. I examine the sweets, the perfumes, the charcuterie, the bottles of Scotch, the cigars.

I don't buy anything. I walk out of Duty-Free. I go over to the newsstand. I cast a quick look over the headlines, I open up a couple of magazines, skim through some tabloids. I leave the newsstand. I take a seat in a metal armchair at Gate 2A. It's not really an armchair, more like a vast row of seats welded to one another; surely to prepare us for the long and close proximity of bodies ahead. I have a sudden urge to call my sister. I want her to know that I'm going to get on the plane, to know which is my flight, just in case something happens. I think back to the November dead. No way to die could be worse than that. This thought soothes me.

I wait forty minutes before boarding the plane. I board the plane. I wait forty-five minutes for takeoff. The man sitting next to me is overweight. His fat brims over the armrest a little.

At the moment of takeoff, my heart rate explodes. In this moment, I'm afraid to die. I say nothing; I think of my childhood; of my grandmother; of the failure of my first love; of the attacks; of Geoffrey Firmin; of my parents and my sister. I look to the wings of the plane for reassurance. The plane is rising.

Do not forget the dream through which you were reborn.

Do not forget your parents.

Do not forget that in your deepest sleep you have accepted the life they gave you.

Do not forget the promise this life contains.

I can't believe I got on this plane. It all seems completely unreal. I look at the little screen in front of me, embedded in the seat: we're now above the Atlantic—just passed over Cape Verde. Six hours and ten minutes down, five hours and twenty minutes to go until São Paulo. I lift the blind on the window to my left. I see some clouds lit by the moon, and the red and white flashing light on the left wing. Everything else is black. We are surrounded by nothingness. My legs are heavy. I want to get up and wander around the plane, but I have to climb over two people to do it. The man on my right snores softly. I give up on the idea of climbing over my neighbors. I can't seem to fall asleep either (horribly agitated). I put on my headphones. I listen to *Le noir de l'étoile* by Gérard Grisey, but I can hardly hear anything. I take off my headphones. I try not to think about the chasm beneath my feet. I don't know why, but I keep thinking of my first love. Why him, why now? To live without him is to feel this vertigo—the vertigo of being suspended hundreds of miles above the heart of the ocean.

Around 1 :00 PM, the smell of chicken fills the airplane. It's dinner time. I unfold my tray table and humbly accept the meal. As the menu indicates (a shiny paper pamphlet was distributed to us by the flight attendants forty minutes after takeoff), we are entitled to a first course of *tartare de tomates et concombre du marché accompagnés de dés de chèvre.* For the main course, a *fricassée de poulet, sauce blanquette et son riz sauvage aux carottes.* For the cheese course and dessert, a slice of camembert and a *cheesecake new-yorkais.* I sniff each dish attentively. I don't taste any of them. I drink all of the little water bottle they give out with dinner—330 milliliters—and then I close my eyes.

I sink back and nod off. I dream that someone is stabbing me between the heart and the shoulder. I don't see my attacker. But the pain is not where the blows land: it surges in my throat, a sensation of burning and tightness in my trachea. I'm woken up by an infant crying at the back of the plane. My initial urge is to strangle it. The exasperation dissolves—I feel the beginnings of empathy.

Chaos is the score upon which reality inscribes itself

Often I think that I want to die more than anything in the world, but that wish is a lie. I understand this when I find myself in an airplane: I don't want to die at all. I struggle to keep my eyes open. My head lolls left and right. My neck is sore. My legs are too long not to be jammed up against the seat in front of me. I close my eyes again. I try to leave this hell.

The plane lands in São Paulo. It's 5:00 AM here, 9:00 AM in Paris, 4:00 AM in Buenos Aires. New security inspections. Customs, then X-rays. I lay my shoes, my jacket, and my bag in large plastic trays (the same ones as Roissy) and I allow them to disappear into the machine. I put my dead cell phone and three coins into a small tray. I'm searched again. Arms armpits stomach legs crotch ankles. I collect my things. I move through the long, empty, windowless hallways. I cut through Duty-Free. A woman is mopping the floor near a display of Lacoste polo shirts. I crave a Brazilian coffee, but all I can find is a Starbucks. I recognize the smell immediately: it's the same smell of cold coffee and icing sugar as in their Paris locations. I don't have any Brazilian money, but that doesn't matter. I ask for an americano in English, then I pay with my credit card. I take a seat at a table. It's identical to the tables in their Paris locations, so much so that for the space of a moment, I have the impression that I never left. Cold air is blowing on my head. I'm underneath an air vent. It's nearly impossible to escape currents of recycled air in planes and airports. I slip on my baseball cap so I don't catch a chill. It's blue and made in Vietnam. It has a Dodgers logo on it, sewn in white.

2

You don't know me.
ARIEL AISENBERG, twenty-one

At 9:40 AM, the plane touches down in Argentina. It all went so quickly. I smile for the first time since yesterday. On the tarmac the air is hot and humid, a strong wind off the river and a smell of kerosene. The sun is harsh. Its whiteness blinds me. My tiredness has become painful. The impression that needles are pricking my brain. I leave the airport. The sky is white, the noise thick. I am plunged once more into the chaos of my childhood.

I get into a black and yellow taxi. The driver greets me without looking back. I see his face in the rearview mirror. He has bags under his eyes. His hair is short and white, plastered with gel. "Where to?" he asks. "The central bus station." A few seconds of silence. Then suddenly,

I have no idea why, he begins to speak, to pour out sentence after sentence in a compulsive Spanish. I make inadequate efforts to keep up with his manic cadence. He says: "I've been working all night . . . My mother told me on the phone *go to bed already!* but my psychiatrist told me *don't sleep during the day, do things, get going again, get some exercise.* I studied chemistry. I had a business that was going very well. The more money I made, the more I thought about taking vacations. I wanted to take advantage of life. I took my wife to Bariloche, Punta del Este, Iguazu . . . Ever been to Iguazu?" "Once when I was really young. I don't remember it." "So anyway, I took my wife around, you know, here and there, and the more vacation time I took, the more I had to trust my business associate. But the bastard betrayed me, he took me for a ride! So I threw him out and then I went bankrupt and then my wife left me—women leave you the minute you fall on hard times, they leave at the worst moment, it's such crap! Now I live at the hotel near the river. My mother offered to let me move in, but how could I? Imagine, at forty-seven . . . No, that's not me, not my way, you can't go back, not like that, and you should of seen her when I said *Mom, the business went under, I lost the house,* you'd of seen her eyes fill with tears for her son . . . My God . . . It kills a man . . . Well, anyway, it's the City Marathon today, see all those people running, with the numbers? I don't know what to think about it—I always look like a monkey when I run, maybe because my belly is too big, who knows, honestly, the other day I was in my car after sitting in traffic for five hours. I was cruising through Palermo . . . and I just broke down . . . I parked the car and started to cry. I cried and I cried, I couldn't stop! D'you know that in six years of driving a taxi, I've never had the same passenger twice? So what, I talk to them, it does me some good. I know that some folks don't like it, but oh well. And anyway my shrink said to me, he told me *Ricardo, stop spending a fortune coming here, you hardly have anything to begin with*, he said to me *go out, talk to people, talk to your family, talk to your loved ones, open yourself up and stop coming to see me.* Would you believe it, I was fired by my own shrink! He told me that when you get right down to it, nothing's wrong with me, nothing serious anyway. I know he's right. I just have to find a woman and get back to hitting the gym. I know some people who are really not doing good. They don't have their health, no family, no work, and me, I have my health, my mother, my cab." The car comes to a halt at a bottleneck on Libertador Avenue. The smell of gas emanates from the trunk; I feel some kind of canister rolling around back there. I open the window. "Anyway, where'd you get in from?" the driver asks, his eyes fixing on the rearview mirror. "From Paris," I answer. "Ah, France! I love France. What's going on with you guys? It's chaos! So terrible. Anyway . . . I take a few pills to stay on the road. This stuff prescribed by my psychiatrist, nothing heavy, you know what I'm saying, just mild, for the insomnia, the nightmares, the crying fits . . . Without it, honestly, I couldn't be driving. Sure, I'm still fragile. But nothing like the last six months. I was crying all the time, over nothing, even just a couple cat hairs on my sweater . . . Where're you going, tell me, which town, somewhere in the provinces?" "To Neuquén." "Neuquén, in Patagonia? You're taking the bus, aren't you? You're in for a day-long trip, at least. I went to Ushuaia a couple years ago. It's breathtaking there! It was my wife, she wanted to see the edge of the world. My *ex*-wife . . . I mean—I still love her. Anyhow, once you've loved that much, you're dead: it's a lost cause. Not an hour goes by I don't think of her . . . Not an hour goes by I don't see her face . . . Christ Almighty, I loved her! Yes, Patagonia, we were cold. We saw the glaciers. That was pretty nice. But, how do I explain this, I wasn't really there, I was somewhere else. What are you supposed to do with an iceberg anyway? And in the end, I found that trip completely depressing. It took me a month to get back on my feet." I try and fail to interrupt him. I want to explain to him that I'm not here as a tourist, that I'm going to my grandmother's funeral and I'm not even sure if I'm going to get there in time because I have no idea what time the funeral is happening. I want to surprise my sister, to surprise my parents. I'd got it into my head that I was going to arrive like the messiah. "We visited one province per year, my wife and I. We went three times to Salta. Then Cordoba. Then El Calafate, and all of Patagonia. But the North-West, that was my favorite. Really good wines up there; the Malbecs are excellent. Oh, did you hear—the Minister of Foreign Affairs has just reestablished all treaties with England, like the Falklands War never happened! God Almighty, who does she think she is? *Las Malvinas* are ours! Here we are, being crushed by the First World. Those self-righteous know-it-alls, I swear . . . Like we're nobodies. This country has everything it needs to succeed, so many natural resources, but we don't exploit them. Take lithium, for example: we have lithium, a lot of lithium, and we sell this raw lithium to China, instead of making factories here and producing the batteries ourselves! Why, why do we do this? Such poverty! In the nineties, a man worked ten hours, got paid a hundred pesos, and with that he bought three loaves of bread; and then he started working twelve hours, still getting paid a hundred, and with that he could buy one loaf of bread; and now he works fifteen hours, *still* gets paid a hundred, and with that can hardly buy a crust of bread. And we wonder why violence is on the rise! Can you believe it?! Look at the protests, only Peruvians in the streets! They come here and steal our jobs and then they complain and parade through the streets, while honest Argentinians like me are working hard to save their skin. And these are the same whiny Peruvians you see on vacation in Necochea getting a nice tan! And me? I'm not in Necochea, I'm working like the devil! I don't have the time to protest, and I sure don't have the money to go to the beach!" I'm struggling to keep my eyes open. The city is vast and fiery. Not a single red light for two kilometers. Skyscraper stickiness savannah. In less than a minute, I watch as we pass a polo field, a football stadium, a racetrack, a gas station. Along the road, palm trees spring out of nowhere: they are there to remind us that beneath the concrete is the growl of the jungle, that she reigns here. One moment the sidewalks are brand new, the next they are dilapidated: no two slabs look alike. Same for the buildings. Same for the faces. It isn't love that needs to be reinvented; it's the very map of the Earth—for this city is not of this world.

*

Traffic jam, again; the taxi stops along the river. I sink piteously into the seat, head thrown backward. My gaze wanders out the window: the monument to the Disappeared looms near the pier, three commemorative black tablets, each more than fifty feet long, forming an open triangle. I discovered this place when I was a child. It has remained, somewhere in my head. Each tablet is crammed with first names, with last names, and with ages, carved in alphabetical and then chronological order, from 1974 to 1977. 8,717 names.

There are some numbers that are evil. Evil thus pierces us algebraically. I know two of the names inscribed on the third and final tablet. Two brothers were taken March 20th, 1977, two hours apart. Ariel Aisenberg, age twenty-one, and Daniel Aisenberg, age twenty-three. I learned of these names from my mother, who was friends with one of them. The first was an arts student and he was taken in the street; the second was studying medicine and was taken from his home. The first died because he loved poetry; the second because his brother loved poetry. To die for a passion; to die for a brother or a sister; a father or a mother; a daughter or a son; for a friend. To die unjustly: nothing is more terrible or more noble. My mother saw Ariel Aisenberg for the last time on March 13th, 1977, at a bus stop on Luis Maria Campos Avenue. She approached him to say hello. He didn't look her in the eye. All he said was, "You don't know me." Ariel Aisenberg, by pretending not to know her, protected my mother. He knew he was being watched; he knew they'd go after anyone seen speaking to him; he knew that he was in danger of torture, maybe even of death. My parents' affliction was not hunger, it was not drugs. It was dictatorship—the gut fear of disappearing. The gut fear of torture. To sleep, during one's whole adolescence, with the window open, in case the soldiers came: to throw oneself into the void rather than endure the electrocutions, the burns, the rapes, the insults. To lose one's friends, thrown alive into the ocean—that's what violence was.

You don't know me

The road opens up little by little. The taxi picks up speed again. The driver talks to me about the next presidential elections; about the brain drain to the rich countries; about Monsanto's GMOs and their fertilizers that are ravaging the fields of the Argentinean provinces. The country is changing, it is at war with the world, and yet internally fractured. There are those who dream of the United States, ashamed of being born to the Third World, and then there are those who dream of a strong and sovereign country. He talks to me about his health, again, then about his mother, then about the wife he loved and his insurmountable sadness. "I hope you will experience that in your life. Pain makes us feel so alive," he tells me, his voice trembling with the first word. I don't risk an interjection to say that I've already lived this sadness he's talking about. The sadness of lost love should never be glorified. It should be covered over. Buried. Eradicated. Always pretend that it's been vanquished. Move forward without looking down at the blossoming abyss. No, I don't know Ariel. No more than I know the dead of Oradour. No more than I know the dead of the Bataclan. I take every liberty with the dead: as though they're not able to avenge themselves. There is something inadmissible about my conduct. I think to myself that it's possible I use them as an opportunity to give my life meaning; that it's possible I use the horrors they experienced to escape the emptiness of my own existence. To finally be able to say to myself: I have a cause to defend. This thought makes me go cold. Sometimes, I hear, *What are you doing taking this on, What are you doing!* You don't know me, said Ariel to my mother. I already said this: he wanted to protect her. But as for me, I hear his words differently, I hear Ariel saying to me, *you can't lay claim to me just because I'm dead*, I hear him tell me, *My death did not give birth to me.*

No, I don't know you.

The taxi drops me in front of the bus station. I give the driver a few hundred pesos without really knowing how much they're worth. He turns his head. "Take care of yourself, yeah? Lots of theft around here." I slam the car door. We will never see each other again.

I go into the station concourse. It's enormous, canopied by a glass ceiling that's probably over a century old. Smell of rubber and soldering. The floor is tiled, terra cotta. I walk toward the screen displaying the departures. I look for Neuquén. Find it. Departure at 11:22 AM, platform eighty-eight. I have forty minutes. I go up to the ticket counter. Four automatic kiosks have replaced the human beings, which suits me fine since I have no desire to speak to anyone. I buy a bus ticket. I pay by card. Children with dirty feet weave this way and that among the travelers. Sometimes asking for something to eat, sometimes asking for money. Their big brothers aren't far, I see them smoking cigarettes, squatting down or leaning against the wall. I walk toward platform eighty-eight. I came to this station a handful of times with my grandmother and my sister. We would sometimes take the night bus to the coast. We spent our vacations in the little house our parents sold in Miramar—there, in the year 2000, terrorists did not exist. Social media did not exist. Twenty-four-hour news channels did not exist. The newspaper was read once a day. We went to the beach. There was the ocean. The surfers. The vendors selling lollipops and the families on vacation. There were also drugs. They poisoned the neighborhood, slowly, surely, while the house fell into disrepair. It was riddled with leaks: the ceilings swelled with humidity, the bedsheets were never dry, the baseboards were swarming with cockroaches. We were forbidden from riding our bikes behind the house: a field had been transformed into the junkies' domain. Our house had been broken into three times, though there was nothing to steal, just shelves full of mildewy books. A fridge from the sixties. Four rust-gnawed bikes. One day, after being away for three months, we found the walls of the bedrooms and the living room smeared with excrement. The smell was like a mix of chlorine and sulfur. My mother cried. A police officer came to assess the damage; he blamed the drug addicts. "They rifle through the cupboards, looking for pills, money, spoons. When they don't find anything, they lash out."

What is it that brings us to the act of destruction; what is it that pushes us over the edge. Not just destitution. Not just exclusion. I see my house again as it was, as if I were there. It had a patio. We hung the laundry out there: in December, it dried in fifteen minutes. We would always find a cockroach in the kitchen sink; we would throw it into the flowerbeds. On the second floor of the house, there was only one room. It was equipped with an old typewriter. That typewriter sat on a termite-eaten desk, next to a sheetless mattress soaked with old coffee stains.

We weren't vegetarians: it wasn't even a question. We ate the meat of the country's herds. We cooked it on broad grills, over charcoal. Its surface was crunchy, charred, but the inside melted in our mouths, the juice ran under our tongues, and from the corners of our lips. My childhood friend was named Fernando. I see him again, in front of the house, a soccer ball at his feet. We would play in his front yard with my sister. He had almond-shaped eyes, like mine, just a little slanted, enough though that the other kids made fun of us: the Chinese, they called us. Fernando had his mother's olive skin, and his father's Russian eyes. He was a fan of River, while Etty and I were fans of Boca. It's possible that Fernando was the first boy I ever loved. He had a grace about him. Fernando died at nineteen from a violent meningitis, the same one that almost took my sister. To die of meningitis at nineteen, can you imagine. Maybe that's worse than dying from bombs or gunshots: no possibility of being made into a hero. Fernando died tritely, assassinated by the arbitrary. Neither my sister nor I went to his funeral. I regret it. And what's more, I don't even know where he's buried. It's likely that his bones lie in a rundown cemetery, somewhere in the suburb of Miramar. There will never be a plaque in honor of Fernando, not like the November dead: his death was not spectacular enough to merit a plaque—I'd even say it wasn't prestigious enough. Who will extol his death? Who will carry on his name? Who will bear his memory? Fernando died in the worst way: he died ridiculously. Not in a great struggle; not from a rare illness; but in a wretched hospital of a wretched illness in a lost province. I was sickened by that poor death, sickened beyond all sickness. Fernando's death would have made anyone doubt the existence of God. It is possible that a part of me renounced my belief in some definitive way, the day of his death—a part, I said.

Still a few minutes to wait. I should have just taken the plane directly to Neuquén: an hour-long flight versus ten hours by bus. Why didn't I think of that? *I should have I could have I would have liked to*—conjugation can destroy you. I lied about the plane: it's not that I forgot to think of it. I was simply afraid to break a habit. I've never made the trip from Buenos Aires to Neuquén by plane. Why change our habits? It doesn't matter if I don't arrive in time for the funeral. I've always disappointed my parents.

My mistake, and so my only possible truth

I haven't known hunger. I haven't taken drugs. I haven't endured torture. For me, violence is limited to images, and to the endurance I require every day just to ingest them—do not give in to the screens. To keep a place in my head, as minuscule as it may be, a place without noise, without restlessness, a place devoid of hatred. For now, books protect me. I've put my faith in them. But the daily temptation of hatred, this temptation to succumb to bitterness and to vengeance, it exists, I feel it—it stirs in all my cells. Books, thought, the stupid beauty of a sky, the comfort of a family—that's all I've found. Relative to the scale of weapons of mass destruction, my remedy is weak.

I'm under twenty-five and I am unable to envision the future. I'm not the only one: we are all fighting like dogs to survive our fear. The world bleeds, and we count the dead. Hatred spreads night and day, there is no respite from the attacks and the massacres, hatred overflows and nourishes the heart of the earth. So sick of watching degradation triumph, sick of seeing the world in tatters, of seeing this world *in extremis* shatter into millions of little bodies sacrificed for nothing.

Life is to burn with the questions

My wounds remain open. I live in a continuum of doubt, subject to the agonizing ordeal of knowing nothing. It's war that asserts itself, downtown, in the suburbs, in the villages, on the trains, in the subways, in the airplanes, beneath the earth, on its surface, in the universities, in the clothing stores, in the restaurants, anytime, anywhere—no one is safe anymore. Violence has metastasized the world, like a cancer secretly putrefies a body. We've let it happen. We didn't understand. And now it's everywhere.

I take a seat on a bench facing platform eighty-eight. I know this bench. I see my grandmother sitting on its edge, her little overnight bag on her knees. My first memory of violence is an utterance—my mother saying a name. That name was violence. I heard it while I was finishing *Huckleberry Finn*, I had ten pages left and

I was obsessed and she said *Ariel Aisenberg* and I said *what are you talking about, Mom* and she said *Ariel my best friend Ariel the disappeared Ariel the tortured the one thrown living into the river Ariel, twenty-one,* and then she said *no one has the right to die thrown handcuffed in the river for their ideas,* I only had ten pages left, but she had to ruin the pleasure of my reading with the return of the dead—the eternal return of the dead, who fall upon us and strike us down.

To be there. To take one's place. To abide. Deep inside what is dying, in the midst of the bullets going astray and the offenses accumulating, in the midst of the misunderstandings imposed on a face other than my own, on a body other than my own, like some kind of special sentence, an excessive initiation into agony. I stay I see I create I listen. To work on the other side of abjection. To work on the other side of vengeance, while the blood continues to flow, while war indiscriminately sacrifices. Human flesh is no longer worth anything. What really matters is not said out loud; it is offered up in the experience of a sentence read, a bolt of lightning at the nape of the neck and in the eyes—in eyes that set themselves upon loving a movement. The power of a word puts an end to ten centuries of torture, the power of a word puts an end to a night of torpor. It is forever to begin again.

To fight the fear of violence, the fear of isolation, the fear of lack. To fight fear. To struggle with finitude in all its forms, perverse and unavowed. To read, to bore into a thousand years of sentences, incessantly, in search of what is inexhaustible, since that's all I have, in spite of time lost, desires in abeyance, the pain that confronts the seer. I told myself a world had to be built—beyond good and evil, beyond the fatal ending point that will impose itself upon me in a fistful of days, beyond the twilight of the destroyers—I promised myself, in the dry darkness of my room, before the coming of the limbo and the dust from which I'm tragically unable to escape, I promised to build a world that thinks, a world that gives, a world that beats—a living world.

I want to be able to fall asleep at night with the feeling of having accomplished something real, something brutally real, beyond the unwavering threat of failure to which we are all subject, to varying degrees. To carry in oneself a knowing, however small, a knowing that exists. I believe that it will never be possible for me to sever myself from the dead. They will be there. They will be lying in wait for me. They will threaten me.

That's the trouble with invisible presences: the more we fear them, the longer they dwell. I hope that my sister dies after me. I hope that everyone I love dies after me. It's possible that those sleepless white nights are so named for the dead who come bearing their cruel light. The bus comes. In the end, maybe it's me who summons the dead—that's a possibility I never imagined. I always say they haunt me. But maybe I call them in my sleep, hoping they'll come find me.

A child approaches me. He's wearing a tracksuit with three white stripes. He extends his hand toward me, cupping his palm. His eyes are a deep and icy black. I slowly fumble through my pockets. I put a little money into his hand. He departs without a word. I have failed at a lot of things since my birth. It is time that I acknowledge it. If I arrive on time for the funeral, I'll say nothing. I'll bring no flowers, no memories. Mad world.

I am starting to wake up.

Frederika Amalia Finkelstein is a French writer and author of two novels: *Forgetting* and *Surviving*. Upon its 2014 release in France, *Forgetting* was met with great critical acclaim and has since been translated into multiple languages. Both have been published in English translation by Isabel Cout and Christopher Elson (Deep Vellum).

Isabel Cout is a translator in Montreal, Quebec. She is currently pursuing graduate work in comparative literature at the Universté de Montréal. Her research explores the themes of emotional ambivalence and social alienation in literature written by descendants of Holocaust survivors.

Christopher Elson has a background in Philosophy and French Studies and holds a doctorate in contemporary literature from Université Paris IV-Sorbonne. He is a member of the joint faculty of the University of King's College and Dalhousie University. He is currently editor of *Dalhousie French Studies* and music columnist for the *Dalhousie Review*. He lives in Halifax, Nova Scotia, with his wife Kate and daughter Lucie.